I0589013

The Criminology Society

J.L. Dumire

J.L. Dumire

This book is a work of fiction. Any characters, events, and dialogue are works of imagination and not to be taken as real. Any resemblance to actual persons or events, living or dead, is entirely coincidental.

The Criminology Society is the intellectual property of J.L. Dumire and not to be used without express permission.

Cover art created by Gloria Byrd of SirenSongsBoutique

Contents

Ten

A special thanks to my parents who
raised me on mysteries
and
to my dearest friends who
supported me as I
continued on this journey.

THE
CRIMINOLOGY
SOCIETY

One

Some call it a glorified book club for the rich and pow-erful. Not entirely correct, as it was founded and frequented by those who *are* well off. But it was not made by those who hold much sway over society. In point of fact, most of the members are thought of as oddballs, or unusual, or at the very least, just over the boundaries of eccentric. Influential, some of them may be, but powerful? My goodness, no. I have known each of them a great many years and can tell you that none of them even have much interest in such things.

Take, for example, Mr Roland Wood, owner, and pro-prietor of the Woodland Company. Easily the most powerful of the members, he owns more land and property than any-one in the business. Many self-made men compliment his prowess in his company, but view him as a weak leader. He doesn't look down on anyone, nor does he rule with an iron fist. Their opinion of him is a typical shortcoming of the true 'rich and powerful'.

He is a very imposing man at first glance. Tall and broad-shouldered with a big brown beard, well-groomed. He looks a bit like an engineer from one of the factories here in Oxford that cleaned up and disguised himself as a member of the upper class. He does have a keen dress sense for such a burly man, always in a fine suit and looking like he is preparing to oversee one of his workplaces. When he smiles, however, he reminds me a bit of Saint Nicholas, with kind eyes and rosy cheeks. Very soft-spoken, but always a looming power waiting behind him, he was the first member of the Society. I met him first when I was at school in America. I can't say why he is a part of this wonderful world of mystery, but he always has an interesting theory when solving a story.

Another member is James Mondey. If one were to describe him then you would assume he would be the very last on the list of people, high *or* low class, to be among those who favour using their brains. He is the second youngest child of a prominent American family, with all the debonair flair of the typical rich playboy. It was no secret that his Dionysian conquests were a constant shame to them. His family could hardly stomach the scandal of disowning him, as '*a Mondey cannot be associated with squalor in any fashion*'. His family pays him a very liberal allowance, to do with as he pleases, so long as he does not associate himself with them. I, myself, have joined him many a night on his prowls for debauchery. Never a dull moment, but always a sense of danger from alcohol or other substances. His involvement in the Society is a great surprise, given how often he is found on the other side of the law. Yet, with enough scotch or brandy in him, he comes up with the most fanciful theories into solving the genius behind the books. He equates to a younger Sherlock Holmes in this way, given that he believes controlled substances give him a higher form of thought. Also, his sharp facial features match the fictional detective's literary description. His cheekbones make me think that many a woman may have cut their frail palms upon them. Also his raven black hair, always combed straight back, until a night of his usual madness leads to it hanging in front of his eyes like a widow's veil.

The next person, or persons, of interest, are Susan Jordain and her personal maid and best friend, Andrea Karras. Like James, Susan comes from a wealthy family, but is the *sole* heiress. The Jordains believe their dear daughter to be a touch too sheltered. She joined the Society out of a lifelong love of intrepid mystery stories. In point of fact, she recently met Agatha Christie and subsequently gave her the idea for her latest novel. Something about a blue train, I believe, but I digress. Miss Jordain was a sickly child and is never very forward, to this day. The first time I met her, she was on the verge of collapse with anxiety due to the crowd around her at a party. She suffers from such panic attacks as this, yet wished to live separate from her family. They always forced her into situations that she was uncomfortable with for the sake of appearances. Tragic. Luckily, they accosted a new maid to aid her. Miss Karras reminds me of James in many ways, as they both vastly enjoy the party scene. If you were to look up the word '*Flapper*' in the dictionary, there would be a portrait of her underneath. The job affords her a decent wage, as Susan insisted on it, but somehow Miss Karras's name manages to open more doors than Miss Jordain's! Miss Karras has friends in all places, which is why she owns such an extensive wardrobe and can access any club in every city. Susan has opened up a considerable amount since knowing Miss Karras these last two years. They have both joined James and I on many occasions. We try to keep it as civil as possible for Miss Jordain's sake, but James and Miss Karras do carry on in such outrageous ways. Susan knows her way around a good mystery, but Miss Karras knows the nature of people, thereby making them both very brilliant in their own ways. Miss Jordain is very fair and fragile with wavy blonde hair whilst Miss Karras is very bold and outspoken for a maid, with dark hair in a bob cut. The only time they seem to be separate is when Miss Karras dances with James or serves to the Society.

Another pair within our little group is the Coles. Professor Spencer Cole, an archaeologist, and historian. And Amelia Cole, the curator of an art museum in Oxford. Despite being based in my hometown, I had never met the two before meeting them in the Society. Both are highly unconventional individuals, beginning with their younger ages in their positions. Spencer became a full professor by his midtwenties through a dissertation given on a discovery with his mentor in Rome. He has a way of seeing through the eyes and thinking through the minds of those who came before us. This translates well into the narratives of fictional characters. He finds it to be a good exercise in the methods he uses to translate the past. His wife, Amelia, is a very liberated woman who takes no sympathy or malice from anyone. She inherited her position from her deceased grandfather, the owner of the museum. Her admiration of art is only rivalled by her admiration of those who made them. She once told me that she fell in love with her husband over a piece of art he had brought to her museum and that it was *her* who proposed to *him!* Unconventional, as I said, but a beautiful love story nonetheless. Her methods differ from his, only in that she uses her artistic imagination to view things in the literary world. Professor Cole is very odd-looking, as he is a young man in an ill-fitting suit, a size or two, too small. He has very soft features that, if not for his wildly unkempt long hair, would have him mistaken for one of the fair folk of Celtic legends. He is always sweeping his sandy blonde locks away to put on his pince-nez glasses. Mrs Cole, as mentioned before, is very modern. Some might say ahead of her time, given her preference for suits, cigars, and taking charge. She refuses to show any weakness, least of all to a man, and does not agree with anyone calling her the '*weaker sex*'. She could never be mistaken for a man with her looks, though. She is a dead ringer for Katherine Dunham with the hair and voice of Josephine Baker all wrapped up in a blue suit. She is the only person alive that I have seen carry themselves more powerfully than Mr Wood.

A touch of an afterthought in the group is our resident police inspector, Cassius Cormac. He's not a bad person, but he is a trifle tiresome. He is so sure of himself and his abilities in detection that he skirts on the side of arrogance. He is not a man from wealthy means, but the others insisted that he join when he asked. We felt it would be a great deal of fun to have a real police inspector in the group, not that he contributes much. He is a charming man with a silver tongue, but a tendency toward crass humour. Inspector Cormac stands quite tall, just under Mr Wood but is lanker, not that one could tell from beneath his long trench coat. He wears well-combed brown hair with sideburns that taper down his jawline, and a thin moustache. I don't know much about him, besides what he tells us, as I don't spend much time with him beyond the Society. Not that I'd care to. He can be friendly enough, but something about him has always rubbed me the wrong way.

Next on our list is the founder of the Society, herself, my aunt the Lady Integra Jilde. I care a great deal for my dear aunt, but between time with the inspector and Lady Jilde, I would choose the inspector anytime. She has always been fond of two things. A good mystery and a good soiree. She and Mr Wood had known one another for a good many years and shared their thoughts on their favourite stories. They both discussed all manner of things behind closed doors. That included the creation of a social group that would enjoy the same intelligent conversations. Many casual members have come and gone, but Mr Wood and my aunt were always at the forefront of the Criminology Society. The two have worked hard collecting the brilliant members that we have. My dear aunt does love the amazing stories shared between brilliant minds and is a delight, but she can also be quite pious and uppity. I commend her for her faith, but as a non-believer myself, I can also understand how it wears thin on others.

And finally, we reach myself. Jonathan Everard. I also love the stories and mental exercises that come with being a member, along with spending time with the many incredible people within. I am not particularly unique in ways beyond my intellect, but I do serve as an aid to my aunt. My parents died when I was at a young age and I have spent most of my life at school or with Lady Jilde. I've always had my own privacy, but my aunt still requires a level of interaction, hence the creation of the Society. My mother and father didn't die from anything suspicious before anyone reading this gets any ideas. It was just an automobile accident, nothing more and nothing less. My appearance is nothing special either. I am average in every attribute you can think of. I favour double-breasted suits, comb my brown hair in a part, and have light blue eyes.

That covers the regular and official members of the Society. Many, as I described before, come and go at their leisure. But with introductions over I believe it is time to begin the story, which began one evening in September. My aunt decided to host an event at her estate. The entire Society was invited to come. Anyone else who wished to attend was welcome to enjoy the ultimate exercise in criminological intellect. A murder mystery party! They were becoming popular at the time, so it was bound to be quite the social event. After all, I aided in setting up the entire party, but I had no idea just how exciting the entire night would get. But I'm getting ahead of things. It began when Mr Wood came for a visit the preceding week.

Two

I was in the lounge, reading the morning paper. My aunt's party had been noted in the society column, to her great pleasure. Lady Jilde was upstairs in the solarium taking her tea when I heard the doorbell out front. The maid, Miss Cyrus would be upstairs serving my aunt and the butler was away on an errand. I folded the paper and laid it on the end table next to me as I got up from the chair and adjusted my vest to go to the door. I glanced out the window from curiosity. The estate sat atop a hill with a beautiful view of Oxford's incredible architecture. I thought many a time about purchasing a telescope to enjoy the view from above a bit closer. But, ever the procrastinator, I always failed to remember until I gazed upon the spires and rooftops again. I shook off these thoughts as I finally reached the door and opened it to a fine dark overcoat. I looked up the towering figure's torso to see none other than Mr Roland Wood on the doorstep.

"Mr Wood!" I said. "Come in, please." I ushered my mentor and friend into the foyer, offering to take his coat for him. He obliged and removed it for me to hang on the coat rack along with his hat. He ran his hand over his brown waves, tidying his hair after the removal of the hat. "So what brings you here, sir?"

"Well, I was in the neighbourhood and thought I would pay a visit before the party this weekend." He smiled cheerfully. "So consider this my RSVP."

"Not as though we needed it," I replied in jest. "We knew you wouldn't miss the event." We had kept it very hush that it would be a murder mystery party. I was still finalizing the details on the mystery itself, so I had hoped that I wouldn't give away anything. Luckily, I have a phenomenal poker face.

"Quite right, too." He chuckled.

"If you'll be in the area on business for the week, we'd be happy to accommodate you." I offered. I had hoped in the back of my head that he would not accept so that I could finish putting together the major event in peace.

"Thank you very much, but no." He held his hands up to me, to my relief. "You know me, I very much prefer a nice hotel. And besides, I'm planning the purchase of a property here in Oxford."

"How wonderful!" My aunt's voice cried from the top of the stairs in a most flamboyant manner. She was in her evening gown and her greying hair was not done up but neatly brushed. Lady Jilde made her way down the staircase with a flourish to greet the family friend. Mr Wood held out his hand to take hers when she made it to the main floor of the foyer, giving it a slight kiss when they met at ground level. "Charming, as always, Roland." Lady Jilde said. "So, do I take it that you'll be moving here then, old friend?"

"Well, not on a permanent basis, you understand." Mr Wood explained. "I'll be buying the place to be my home when I'm in town, but when I am away, I thought it might be a regular meeting place for the Criminology Society."

"Oh! Splendid!" Lady Jilde exclaimed with a clap of her hands. "Come, and tell us more!" She gestured him into the lounge and directed attention back to the top of the stairs. "Oh, Essie, dear. Please fetch some tea for Mr Wood, won't you?" Miss Cyrus nodded from the top of the staircase and slipped away to retrieve the kettle. In the lounge, the three of us took our seats and continued our conversation. "I very much enjoy the idea of a meeting place for us all to spend our time!"

"Yes," I interjected. "I think that it would be a welcome change from this same old lounge all the time.

"Well don't take this to mean that I don't adore your home, but my thoughts exactly!" Mr Wood smiled, making the curls of his moustache turn inward. "Something to expand our levels of ambience."

"Especially given that the Coles never allow us to enter their abode." Lady Jilde turned her nose up a bit. She had nothing against the Coles, but they were very secretive about their home.

"My lady, you have to understand that their work is very sensitive." Mr Wood explained. "They take care of highly delicate artefacts and artwork."

"Oh, that's true, I suppose." She sighed.

"And I doubt that you'd want to see the dwelling of Mr Mondey." Lady Jilde sneered with a shudder.

"*Sodom and Gomorrah.*" She shivered again. I stifled a laugh, knowing full well what she meant. It was true. Any place that James stayed was usually a revolving door of sexual partners.

"Ultimately, this is a brilliant change I'd say." I attempted to change the subject for the sake of my aunt, still fighting back my laughter. "We'll have our own little designated home away from home."

"Indeed."

"So, we'll be seeing you at the event this weekend?" Lady Jilde draped herself across the sofa in her usual extravagant fashion.

"Yes, indeed, my lady." Mr Wood replied. "I would never miss an event planned by you."

"Actually, while it was my idea, the mind behind the planning is my darling nephew." She presented her hands as though a curtain had come open to reveal me. Miss Cyrus came in with the tea and placed it on the table between the seats, beginning to pour.

"How extraordinary." Mr Wood glanced my way, accepting the cup from the maid. "Thank you, Essie." She nodded her head with a smile and continued to pour for myself and Lady Jilde.

"I only hope to give the experience of a lifetime with the plans I have made for the event." I explained, taking a sip of my tea.

"I'm sure you will. I read about it being the biggest event of the year in the society page only this morning." Mr Wood placed his cup on the table and crossed his legs. "I only hope you'll make the mystery a challenging one." He said with a knowing grin on his face. I sputtered a bit.

"How did you know it would be a mystery game party!?" I was in awe. I made no reference or clue to the plans of the evening.

"I had an inkling." He chortled. "You forget, my boy, that I was *also* the founder of this Society." I laughed in amusement, not being able to contain it. I shouldn't have been as surprised as I was, given that I knew full well how clever he is. He reached into his vest and pulled out his fob watch, glancing at it. "Well, I'd do best to get out of your hair so that you can continue with building this perfect mystery." He got back up with a pat on his knees.

"Oh, must you go?" Lady Jilde leaned in his general direction. "You've only just arrived."

"Indeed, but my social call was only to visit and let you know I'd be in for the weekend." He pocketed his watch and buttoned his jacket. "I have a bit of business to attend to in Eynsham."

"Well, at least allow me to show you to the door." I asked Mr Wood. He agreed and we both retrieved his hat and coat.

"I think it'll be very ambient this weekend." He said, cryptically.

"Oh?"

"I can smell it in the air." He explained. "There's going to be a storm."

"We're almost a week out, how can you tell so soon?" I laughed.

"Just a little of that country boy talent from my youth." Mr Wood placed on his hat and gave me a wink before leaving the manor. I gave my cheek a scratch and reentered the lounge with my aunt.

"Well, I'll have to work extra hard to surprise Mr Wood it would seem." I said to her.

"Talking of surprises, have you prepared the other little details that I suggested, dear nephew?" She leaned forward in her seat, wearing a serious expression across her face.

"Yes." I nodded. "Don't worry. I didn't leave anything to chance this weekend." I was confident that the whole evening would go according to plan. I always had a handle on my emotions but I could feel a swell of excitement within me. "Oh, I'd best go and prepare the payments for the servants."

"Ah, no need, Jonathan, I've already handled it myself." She took another sip of her tea, but something about the way she looked as she did so didn't sit right. Thinking back, I should have paid it more heed at the time. Several lives may have been spared had I asked her then what she meant.

Three

The eve of the party finally came on Saturday and Lady Jilde was in rare form. She sat at her vanity, preparing her makeup and clothing for her lavish evening of being hostess to some of our prestigious friends. As for myself, I was already dressed to receive and was looking over the final preparations for the party. Before going into the kitchen, I looked out the same window in the lounge and noticed that the evening sun was hued to a burnish orange. As the evening colour set in it was being overshadowed by a grey cover. Mr Wood was right! Not that I was surprised, knowing his cleverness. There is definitely something to be said for coming from a lesser background than being born in advantage. Before turning my back to the window I noticed the gardener out front, on his way down the hill. He seemed to be avoiding the main drive and went straight over the hill with his wheelbarrow full of tools. The only assumption that I could think of at that time was that he was going to trim the foliage at the base of the hillside like we'd asked him to do for two weeks. I shrugged it off because I had much more to do at the time. I hurried off to the kitchen to check the menu for the evening.

I wasted no time, with so much to do and the guests soon to arrive, I quickened my pace but stopped suddenly at the door. I pressed my ear against it because I thought I heard something odd. Laughter? Perhaps more of a giggle. I knew all too well what that meant. I pushed open the door to find my dear friend James Mondey, a complete mess, flirting with the cook.

"James." I raised my brow. His tie was hanging from his open collar, his hair was completely dishevelled and his current suit was almost a shambles. "Please let Mrs Langley get back to preparing the food for this evening. With extra emphasis on the *Missus*." The cook was a woman of middle age and married, not that either of those things would deter James. He sought out any and all kinds of debauchery, the more dramatic the better. Mrs Langley was attractive for her age, her most eye-catching feature being her bright red hair which stood out against her all-white uniform. The apron was flecked with food stains from her hard work on the small banquet we had planned. Her husband was Mr Langley, the gardener, who was a lazy man, as I alluded to earlier. It makes perfect sense why she'd be so taken with lively, young, and handsome James Mondey.

"But Jonny, I can't help myself around a gorgeous woman such as this." He ran his thumb across Mrs Langley's cheek. I rolled my eyes and walked over to the sink, taking a cup and running some cold water in it.

"What did I say about calling me '*Jonny*'?" I simply poured some of the cold water over his head. He gave a slight cry over the temperature which turned to amused laughter. "The only reason I did that is because the hose doesn't reach in here." Mrs Langley let out a giggle herself.

"Very funny, Jon." He used the damp to slick back his hair.

"What brought you so early?" I asked my friend. "The party isn't for another two hours which means everyone will be here in one."

"Ah, yes, the fashionably early crowd." He chuckled. "Truth be told, I took a cab here."

"I rather surmised that from the lack of a car in the driveway." I gestured over my shoulder, pointing at the front door. "What happened to yours?"

"Not sure." He replied. "I woke up outside a pub I didn't remember and both my date and my motorcar were missing. So all in all I guess I had a fun evening last night." His passive shrug was almost comical. "I came so soon because I wondered if I could borrow a suit and clean myself up."

"Ha, of course." I gestured him out front to the foyer so that we could head upstairs and get him looking presentable. "So, you took a cab to get here?" I asked.

"Sure did. At least she left me my wallet." He replied with

a boisterous laugh. We came to a sudden halt when we came in contact with Lady Jilde.

"Ah, Mr Mondey." My aunt pursed her lips and forced a smile toward James. "I see you've arrived early." She was dressed to the nines with her blue evening dress with white trim and boa. She was also in her matching blue turban hat with silver feathers and a cigarette holder in her hand, waiting for a cigarette.

"I'd say fashionably but obviously I need help in that area." He joked about his appearance. He knew it wouldn't be in his favour, but anytime he could tease my uppity aunt was a treat for him.

"Yes, quite." She slid past us. "Well, I do believe I'll head down to see what else needs doing, while you, Jonathan, help Mr Mondey to become halfway presentable." She finished descending the stairs and sauntered off to the dining room.

"I think she's warming up to me." James stated.

"Oh?"

"Yeah, she seemed less disgusted and I only have a little bit of frost on my shoulder this time." He let out another laugh, which I reciprocated.

We retired to my room where I began digging through my closet. I was already wearing my double-breasted blue suit with the red silk tie, so I thought he might make use of my white three-piece. I picked out a selection of ties for him to choose from and draped them across the back of my desk chair. I glanced over my desk to be sure that I had no clues left on it from my party plans. Luckily, I had cleared it before anyone had arrived but double-checking is always a good contingency. I could hear water running in the washroom as James freshened himself up.

"Jon? Do you mind if I borrow some of this cologne you have in here?" He called in.

"Help yourself. It's for the best that you not smell of booze until at least half an hour into the party." I chuckled. "I laid out a suit for you along with some ties."

"Oh, I think I'll only need one." James joked. I was unaware at the time of his entry into the room without apparel, until I turned around with a retort of my own.

"Ever the comedian, my-*God in Heaven!*" I averted my eyes to the ceiling! "James, have you no shame?"

"Not really." He shrugged, beginning to dress right in front of me. "It was good enough for Adam and Eve."

"James, you have never set foot in a church and if you did you'd likely burst into flames." I knew for a fact he didn't know a lick of that story. He wasn't atheistic, but he preferred the dominion of the Greek pantheon.

"Highly likely." He buttoned up the shirt and put on the vest, finally covering himself with the trousers.

"I'm going to head back downstairs and finish looking things over while you get dressed." He waved me out and I went back down the decorative hallway, returning to the staircase. I could hear my aunt speaking to someone. I had assumed it was Miss Cyrus, but upon reaching the bottom of the steps and looking into the lounge, I found I was mistaken. Inside, with Lady Jilde, were the Coles.

"Oh, nephew! Look who's arrived!" She smiled. The pale professor smiled, wearing a snug tweed suit around his lithe body, and waved.

"*Monsieur* Jonathan!" Mrs Cole called out. She was wearing an excellent blue square-button suit and an arrow collar shirt. Her raven black hair shone with Brilliantine and her smooth ebony skin dimpled with her kind face. "*Merveilleux de te voir mon ami!*"

"Wonderful to see you as well Mrs Cole." I bowed as she shook my hand.

"Jonathan, how many times?" She shook her head in response. "Just call me Amelia."

"I still favour to stand on ceremony, I'm afraid." I explained. "You two are usually the last to arrive."

"Yes." The Professor interjected. "We only have a few things to finish on our current project. We'll be unveiling a new exhibit at the museum for the Greek-Roman differentiation."

"Well, have a seat!" Lady Jilde exclaimed. "We must make this party a joint celebration for this." My aunt snapped her fingers and directed Miss Cyrus to serve drinks. Miss Cyrus carried over a silver tray of champagne and held it out to the guests. Lady Jilde picked one up, as did Mrs Cole.

"N-none for me, thanks, Essie." Spencer denied as he and his wife took a seat on the couch. The two of them continued to explain the details of the exhibit and the gala we would all be invited to upon opening.

"The exhibit is a show of compared art between Ancient Greece and the Roman Empire." Professor Cole began describing. Mrs Cole took a drink, looking at her husband with admiration as his passion for history began to rise. "Imagine, if you will, corridors where you can see two cultures so similar, but learn just how different they were, too!" The professor was so giddy that his leg was bounding.

"I doubt I could tell the difference, myself." Lady Jilde chuckled.

"That's what this exhibit is for." The professor replied.

"*En effet* and this will be a wonderful addition for the students of the university. The ones who study both the history *et* the mythology of both cultures." Mrs Cole added to her husband's excitement. She was correct in her description. The exhibit's usefulness would be invaluable.

"As you can tell, I'm quite eager for this release." Cole contained his childlike eagerness by clasping his hands together and locking them between his knees. "I will be one of the credited professors giving lectures on some of the amazing architectural pieces. But Amelia will be the primary keynote speaker!"

"That's marvellous!" I exclaimed.

"*N'est-ce pas?*" She held up her glass which my aunt met with her own. "*Salut!*"

"Here, here." Lady Jilde chuckled.

The bell out front rang and I excused myself to go to the foyer, nearly bumping into the butler, Harold Isaac. He was an elderly gentleman and the most typical kind of butler you can imagine. Diligent, trustworthy, and even a man of decent humour. He was my height, always at attention, with white hair and a beard, along with some small round glasses.

I had acquired much of his help in setting up our mystery. He would even be the one to play our victim for the evening! Our near-collision seemed to give him a start.

"Oh, my!" He placed his hand over his chest. "Master Jonathan. Do allow me, I don't want to feel like an antique yet."

"Of course, Mr Isaac." I chuckled. A rumble of thunder came as the door opened and out front was Inspector Cormac. The inspector came in with a gust of wind, holding his trench coat shut with one hand and his fedora hat down with the other.

"Blimey!" He exclaimed. "Where the hell did that come from? One minute, I'm driving along, slightly cloudy, and the next I'm getting blown to pieces with the leaves!" He removed his hat and handed it off to Mr Isaac along with his coat. He wore a plain brown suit, nothing too special given a policeman's pay.

"Yes. Mr Wood warned me that he thought the weather would turn tonight. But I think it'll lend to the ambience of the evening." I said with a similar smile to the one Lady Jilde gave James.

"That would've been nice information *before* driving out here." The inspector huffed.

"And not get a dose of your sour persimmons, Inspector?" James called as he descended the staircase. "It just wouldn't be a Criminology Society event without at least one of your patented complaints!" He laughed.

"Very funny, Mondey." His moustache crooked at the sides of his mouth, betraying the faint smile of humour. "Early rather than late for a change, eh?" His cockney drawl spat out.

"This time it was arrive early or not at all." James and Cormac both entered the lounge.

"Ah, Cassius! James!" The professor sprung up, shaking the men's hands. "Surprising to see you both so soon."

"That's what I was just saying to the walking decanter over here." Cormac patted James's back roughly.

"I'll have you know, I'm currently sober as a judge, but intend to rectify that immediately." He gestured over to Miss Cyrus, who brought him the serving tray of drinks. "Thanks, Essie." Mrs Cole offered the others one of her cigars, which the inspector gladly partook in. I would have taken my seat, but eager to play the host, stayed next to the entrance to the foyer when I noticed the arrival of another car. A white sports model that I recognized as Miss Jordain's vehicle, most likely driven by Miss Karras.

"Mr Isaac." I signalled him to be prepared to open the

doors for the dear ladies. We didn't want them blowing about like the inspector. He readied himself and stood, hand on the door, waiting to open at the first sound of footsteps. The sound popped up and Mr Isaac swung open the door, allowing the ladies to come running in to beat the storm!

"Mr Isaac! Oh, prompt as always!" Miss Jordain paid the elderly butler a compliment. She was covered from head to toe in beautiful white. Her fur-collared coat was taken from her shoulders by Miss Karras and handed to Mr Isaac. He also insisted on taking up her coat as well, but Miss Karras declined.

"Miss Andrea?"

"I may be a guest tonight, but I'm still a domestic." She smiled. "I can hang my own coat."

"You are also a lady." Mr Isaac held out his hand. "Allow me to treat you as such." Miss Karras gave a small giggle.

"Very well, Mr Isaac." She removed her own coat and handed it to him.

"Thank you, my dear." Mr Isaac said as he turned on his heel to hang the coats in the closet.

"Come with me, Miss Jordain." I gestured. The sound of rain began pattering everywhere. "Wow, you two made it in just in time." I chuckled. When the ladies ran in, Miss Karras even had an umbrella, which may very well come in handy when leaving.

Entering the lounge, everyone looked at Miss Jordain like she was an angel in her gorgeous white party dress, coupled with her waves of blonde hair. Her dress also shone in places with gems along the sash belt around her waist. The professor seemed to lose his breath the moment he saw her and the inspector choked on his cigar, to my great amusement.

"Susan! You look *merveilleux!*" Mrs Cole exclaimed. Miss Karras followed in after her mistress and friend. If Miss Jordain looked like an angel, her maid looked like a little devil. Clad in a black and gold flapper's dress, with a feathered headband adorning her bobbed hair. "As do you, Andrea."

"Well." Lady Jilde spoke up. "Miss Karras's clothes hardly seem appropriate for a woman in a service capacity."

"But I *am* providing a service." Miss Karras said in her cockney drawl. My aunt raised her eyebrow as if waiting for an explanation. "Susan insisted." She smiled. Miss Jordain nodded in agreement. "The invitation listed me as a guest, after all." Lady Jilde rolled her eyes and stood up.

"I suppose that will have to stand, but I suggest we all adjourn to the dining area until Mr Wood arrives." Lady Jilde suggested. I looked at my watch and if we didn't begin dinner, we'd be running very late into the evening indeed. Mr Wood is exceptionally punctual, so I couldn't factor why he hadn't arrived yet.

Everyone seemed quite eager to have dinner as it was nearly approaching six o'clock. Knowing Mr Wood, he would hardly mind. Punctual, he may be, but an addict to his work he is, also. I wasn't too worried about things beginning too soon. Dinner would be the start of the mystery, but before announcing dinner, I needed to go find out from the cook if it was prepared. I slipped from the gathering and walked hurriedly to the kitchen.

"Mrs Langley?" I asked. She turned her attention from the oven, covered in flour from baking the dessert. "How has dinner progressed?"

"Check for yourself." She waved me over to the stove. On the top was a splendid smelling soup. I grabbed a spoon and dipped it into it, taking a careful sip. Amazing! Savoury, spicy, and a wonderful accompanying tang to finish off! I have no idea what it was, but I knew it would be a hit with the guests!

"How is it that you managed to put a piece of Heaven in this?" I asked her.

"Ha! Heaven is in this dessert. I put Something else special in the soup." She laughed. "That ought to stick to their hoity-toity ribs. Could you tell Harold and Essie the stuff can be served anytime?"

"Excellent." I left the kitchen and relayed the instructions to the others, reentering the lounge. "Dinner is ready, everyone." I announced.

"Shouldn't we wait for Mr Wood?" Asked the professor.

"The food will keep. In fact, I'm sure he may be planning his own surprise." I said. Thinking over it, he may be planning to add something to my event to key it up. He was welcome as he is a clever man.

Everyone flowed into the dining room across from the lounge. The long table would fit two more people than accommodated with a beautiful runner spanning the length of it and skirting from the ends. The wallpaper was the same floral red that we had in the lounge with a fantastic mould meeting it with the ceiling and floor. A gorgeous chandelier of similar design to the foyer, but smaller, hung at the direct centre of the table. The guests took their places and awaited the arrival of the wonderful dinner we were to expect. Mr Isaac and Miss Cyrus came in with trays of everyone's servings. I glanced over to my aunt, saying grace for herself as the bowls were doled out. Grace, or none, aside, we all dug in with rave reviews on Mrs Langley's skill as a chef!

"Cor, this stew's bloody amazing!" Cormac exclaimed.

"I'd have to concur." Professor Cole agreed with the, albeit crude, commendation. "Mrs Langley has outdone herself tonight!"

"I'll say!" Miss Karras dabbed her mouth with her napkin. "If it's not too forward, can I ask what the dessert will be?"

"Ever the sweet tooth, Andrea." James laughed, garnering a cute chuckle from Miss Jordain.

"Always, Jimmy-boy." Miss Karras laughed back. Lady Jilde cleared her throat, hoping for the raucous conversation to quiet down. I decided to ease the tension by answering Miss Karras's valid question.

"To answer your question, it's a special cake that I asked Mrs Langley to prepare." I stated. "A cinnamon and almond cake that is beyond comprehension." I could almost taste it already!

"It has been Jonathan's favourite ever since we brought on the Langleys." My aunt laughed in her throat.

Once the dessert course was finished, and I was sure everyone had sufficiently helped themselves, I glanced over to Mr Isaac. He nodded and stood by the kitchen door. I wiped my mouth with my napkin and stood at my table placement.

"Everyone," I stated. "If you would, please look under your chairs." Everyone looked quite confused, except my aunt, who was eager for the reactions. "Under them, you'll find a card, which will portray who you are in the game we are about to partake in. Please do not show this card to any of the others." I explained. The guests look very quizzical and some almost concerned.

"Who made these, then?" Inspector Cormac questioned.

"Ah, that would be me." Lady Jilde interjected. It was true, she had made them for my event. In fact, she'd given me the idea to use identity cards. A way of keeping track of who the murderer was and how to solve it with my set clues. I reached down and retrieved my own card, looking at it and smirking at what I was given.

"We will be solving a mock murder, which should be easy enough for us. I've planned out the entire concept to the letter and will be guiding you." I continued.

"But won't this give the investigators an edge?" Mrs Cole asked.

"No, because according to my card, I am '*The Narrator*'." A perfect fit for the story now, isn't it? "I merely serve as a guide."

"That so?" The Inspector huffed. "Not so sure this is very tasteful."

"It's all in good fun, Inspector." James laughed. "Like all the books!"

"What I want to know is, who is playing the victim here?" Miss Karras spoke up.

"Good question." I said. "Mr Isaac?" The butler cleared his throat and was about to give the performance of his life when a choking sound filled the room. Even I was puzzled.

We all turned our attention to the sound. Inspector Cormac was choking violently! Everyone clamoured to his aid, but it was to no avail. Within moments, Inspector Cormac fell to the floor, dead. A look of pain on his face and a card in his hand. The card read, '*The Victim*'. And so began the game of mystery that would determine the fate of the Criminology Society.

Four

Inspector Cassius Cormac lay dead on the dining room floor. It didn't seem real. We were all aghast with a terrible feeling of dread. Someone... Someone *here* had murdered a policeman! But why? We all stood in stunned silence, staring at the body. The only sound around us was the sound of rain and thunder from outside. It surrounded us as though we were in the eye of a great storm, cutting us off from the rest of the world. Mr Isaac was still at attention in the corner but was just as taken as we were.

"Mr Isaac!" Lady Jilde broke the silence, startling Miss Jordain and the Professor. Mr Isaac shook off his surprise and looked to his aged employer. "Don't just stand there, phone the police!" She pounded the table with her palm. Mr Isaac sprung into action and left the dining room to make the call.

"My Lord." Professor Cole cupped his hands around his mouth. "What do we do in this scenario?" He asked.

"If I could make a suggestion?" James chimed in. We all looked to him, except my aunt, who rolled her eyes. "I believe we should all vacate the dining room and wait in the lounge for the authorities to arrive." He waved his hands as he talked. Mr Isaac left the dining room first to reach the telephone.

"I'm surprised. A very level-headed thing to do." Lady Jilde said with condescension in her voice. James gave her a patronizing bow and everyone began leaving the dining room. We all were careful to avoid disturbing the body or anything at the table.

Everybody managed to stagger into the foyer to go into the lounge, but we were stopped short. Before we could enter it Mr Isaac gestured us to a halt. He looked very sombre and it looked to me like everybody could feel it.

"I have bad news." He said. I could see Miss Cyrus looking around the corner of the dining-room door. "The phone lines appear to be down, possibly due to the storm." Hearing this, Miss Jordain began to hyperventilate.

"Hang tight, Miss." Miss Karras took ahold of the faint young lady.

"Steady on." Mrs Cole added, also coming to our friend's aid.

"B-b-but, I- we..." She began tearing up and her voice was cracking as she stuttered.

"Take a moment, Miss Jordain." I said. I pointed her to the stairs. "Take one of the rooms upstairs to have a breath."

"Um, nephew, dear?" Lady Jilde spoke up. "Wouldn't it be prudent for us all to stay together, rather than let anyone out of sight?"

"Not when one of our friends is on the verge of a breakdown." I urged. "You two know where the guest rooms are." I waved Miss Karras on. She nodded in thanks to me and began helping her mistress up the stairs.

"I don't like leaving anyone alone in my house right now, Jonathan." Lady Jilde snapped under her breath.

"It was better to just let the poor girl torture herself? She was just as shaken up as the rest of us." I stood my ground, to her surprise. I usually indulged her bouts of selfish preferences, but this was someone else's mental wellbeing we were talking about. Was it wise to send them off? Maybe not, but I was not going to turn a blind eye to my friend's anxiety.

"Talking of torture." James chimed in. "Where on earth is Roland?" He asked. Lady Jilde and I both looked at him, perturbed.

"Surely, you don't thank that Mr Wood-" I began.

"No, no! Don't misunderstand me!" He defended himself. "I'm more concerned for *his* safety as well."

"I'm sure." Lady Jilde sneered.

"My lady?" James said in a saccharine tone. My aunt turned to him with her fake smile. "Shove that attitude someplace we don't have to see or hear it." She gasped and I was taken aback by his sudden show of boldness. He's teased her behind a veil of humour before, but this was quite different! "I'm trying to think of *everyone's* safety, while *you're* worried about the privacy of your house."

"Thinking of something other than yourself or alcohol, forgive me if I don't take you seriously." She scoffed.

"Enough!" Mrs Cole shouted with a large cloud of cigar smoke billowing out. "Infighting will solve nothing!" She maintained a haughty composure, displaying her dominance.

"And how do we avoid infighting, my dear, when there is clearly a killer amongst us?" Lady Jilde suggested.

"We don't know that, yet." Professor Cole stated, brushing his sandy blonde waves out of his eyes. "It could still have been caused by an outside source."

"Oh, *please!*" Lady Jilde was adamant. "We all discuss methods to kill people from books on a regular basis! And do we really think that nobody here had a motive for him?"

"He was a policeman, milady. What would any of us gain

by killing a policeman?" Mrs Cole took another puff of her cigar. "Unless you know something we don't." Her glare was so intense that she might have knocked Lady Jilde over with her eyes. We were all confused, but tensions were high. My aunt just avoided the powerful woman's gaze and we all finally took some of the stress from our feet by tucking into the lounge. James started by knocking back a couple of drinks and pacing the end of the room.

"I'd say, the first thing to do is for us to figure out how to make contact with the outside." James pointed out.

"The most prudent thing would be for someone to go and get the police themselves." I said.

"And what if the murderer is the one who leaves?" Lady Jilde spat.

"*Probable*, they would skip town and, therefore, be known as the killer." Mrs Cole explained. "*Par cette logique*, we would all, then, be safe." Lady Jilde turned away, having run out of arguments for the situation.

"Well, I would gladly go, but my car has gone missing." James explained, taking a gulp of the drinks from before.

"I think the thing that should be done first is to try going to the guest rooms." I suggested. The others looked at me with strange expressions. "That way, we will not have any reason to distrust one another so long as we stay in our appointed rooms. The ladies, upstairs, are already safe in one themselves. And we will have Mr Isaac and Miss Cyrus keep an eye on the hall to prevent anyone from trying anything while one of us retrieves the police." The group looked to one another and nodded in a precarious agreement. Except for my dear, stubborn, aunt.

"Why do you think I would trust them? They are hardly above suspicion, themselves!" Lady Jilde fussed.

"My lady." Mr Isaac bowed. "I can assure you that I have nothing to hide from you. And I will gladly vouch for Miss Cyrus, as she was never out of my sight this evening." Lady Jilde shuffled in her dress and begrudgingly agreed.

"That still leaves the question of who should go." She grumbled.

"If James wishes to go, I'll give him the use of our car." I said, nodding to him. We hurried into the foyer where Miss Cyrus stopped us, draped in raincoats.

"Wait!" She said. "You'll be waterlogged out there." She held out the coats for us.

"Thanks, Essie." James said, pouring on his patented charm once again. Professor Cole ran into the foyer alongside us.

"Um, E-Essie? Do you happen to have another raincoat on hand?" He asked.

"You plan on coming, too, Spencer?" James asked. "Wouldn't think you the type."

"Oh, I-I'm not. But if we'll be here for a while, I have something in our vehicle that I need." He explained.

"I see. Alright, let's away!" James and I both hurried out into the heavy rain and rolling thunder to retrieve the car. The wind nearly parachuted my coat and I felt like I might fly away! Luckily, James had ahold of my coat's collar, pulling me along as we approached the garage at the leftmost side of the house. Why we exited by the front door was beyond me, as the garage was just outside of the kitchen. My own fault, I suppose. James was following me. Writing this, I feel a bit mortified, but none of our heads were on right at the time, so judge accordingly. We managed to duck into the garage and shook ourselves off from the rain.

"I haven't seen it come down like this in a while." I said. "If the party had continued it would've made for some terrific ambience."

"Yes, and I could be curling up with some brandy and a few warm bodies." James chuckled again. I shook my head.

"Even in the face of danger, James?" He let out a mock hero's laugh. He took off the coat and threw it on the floor of the passenger's side, so as not to ruin the upholstery. He shook his head once more and slicked his wet hair back, climbing into the car. He started it up with a chug and an echoing bang from the exhaust. We covered our ears from the painful pop of backfire in the enclosed space.

"You sure you won't come, too, Jonny?" He asked.

"My home, my responsibility." I shrugged. I patted his shoulder and closed the car door. I moved in front of the car and began reeling the garage gate open. The headlights came on in a flash and the car bypassed me with a rev as it set out into the rain.

I promptly shut the gate and ran back out of the door into the storm. I would have gone back in through the kitchen door but, knowing Professor Cole, the timid man may need some assistance retrieving what he was after. I am much taller and built than he is, therefor if I nearly flew away, he would be like that of a fall leaf. I ran back to the front of the manor and, sure enough, there was the professor... Stuck in his own car... Headfirst... I could only make out his flailing legs and the flowing tail of the raincoat blowing in the wind beside the open door of the Coles' car. Running up to the car, I tried to get ahold of his stick-like ankles to save my face from the heels of his button shoes. He let out a high shriek of surprise.

"Calm down, Professor, it's just me!" I shouted over the wind and rain.

"Oh, thank the Lord! Pull me out, Jon!" He pleaded.

"What happened!?" I couldn't fathom how he'd managed to get into such an awkward position, even if his property were gold bricks!

"Some debris hit the door and knocked me in! I'm begging you, I'm becoming claustrophobic!" His legs began kicking again and I took a risk and grabbed him by the back of the coat collar and pulled! We both came tumbling out of the car and fell into the driveway with a splash!

"Come, now! We need to get inside!" I called. The professor hurried to pick up a suitcase before it got too wet and we both ran like mad to the front door! In our haste to come in, we took a spill on the smooth flooring and the water that blew in with us. I came crashing down backwards while the professor swooped over me, spinning over to keep from landing on his suitcase! Knowing how fragile he is I scrambled to check on him. "Professor! Are you alright?" He was clinging to his suitcase and seemed a bit stiff. The only reply was a weak wheezing sound and a twitch in his eye.

"Ouch." He managed to squeak through gritted teeth.

"Spencer!" Mrs Cole exclaimed. She ran in with Miss Cyrus, kneeling down next to me. Everyone else had already been escorted to their respective rooms by Mr Isaac. Except for Mrs Cole, who insisted on waiting for her husband. "Are you hurt?" She asked with intense worry.

"I'm alright, my love." He sighed. "Jonathan? Could you give my wife and me one moment?" Professor Cole spoke, crackled.

"Sure thing." I assured him. I gave my raincoat to Miss Cyrus and opted to begin heading up the stairs to my own room to dry myself and change into some less sopping clothes. As I crested the stairs, however, I couldn't help but overhear a conversation between the Coles.

"*Vous avez présenté toute l'affaire?*" Asked Mrs. Cole.

"*J'ai dû. Je n'ai pas pu le trouver dans la tempête.*" The professor replied. I couldn't help but hug the wall a bit and bend my ear to the conversation. They never conversed in Mrs Cole's native tongue unless they had something to hide. The last time I heard them speak in French was to keep my aunt's surprise birthday party a secret. I knew something was suspicious about this. If I had continued studying French at school, I might have understood better. I swapped to Spanish, for reasons I would rather not discuss here.

"*Vous ne pensez pas qu'il est un peu risqué de tout emporter avec vous? Autour de tant de monde?*" I only recognized one word that the professor's wife said. She was asking him about the risk of something he brought in. But what?

Before I could go any further with my suppositions, I decided to vacate the landing so that I wouldn't be caught eaves-dropping. Also, due to the increasing discomfort of being in a soaked suit. I hurried down the empty hall and entered my room with an easy nudge of the door. My first order of business was to go into my washroom and towel off my hair. I changed out of my suit and walked across my floor to the closet. I put on a clean shirt and thought I'd do well to get comfortable. I put on my leisure trousers and matched them with my blue smoking jacket.

Once I had closed the jacket, I took a moment to look out of the window. I could see nothing out of it except for the horizontal rain streaking across the glass. I could only see any further when lightning flashed and turned the night into day in a blink. There wasn't much to see. Just the side yard and the trees running alongside the hedges. The sudden flash, and subsequent thunderclap, made me drop the curtain. I pulled it shut in the hope of dulling the sound. I had to rub my eyes from the flash of lightning and walked back to my writing desk. Slumping down into my chair, I couldn't help but be concerned for James's safety in this storm. I opted to look into one of my drawers and found the banner I intended to hang up to congratulate whoever solved the mystery. I was deep in thought over what this evening had become when I heard a thump in the next room. I wouldn't have thought much of it but I realized that was one of the guest rooms!

I ran back into the hall and looked up and down the empty corridor. Nothing there, so there was no mistaking where the sound came from. I ran up to the room to the left between my own and the solarium. In my haste, I pounded on the door!

"Is anyone in there?" I called. The sound of a struggle rattled out! "I'm coming in!"

"No, don't!" Miss Karras's voice came from the other side.

"Miss Karras?"

"Yes, and Miss Jordain is not, um, decent. So to speak." Miss Karras explained.

"Is she, at least, feeling better?" I asked.

"One moment, Jonathan!" Miss Jordain bid me. I waited a moment, confused. A short time after, the door opened to Miss Jordain on the other side. She looked quite dishevelled, her makeup smeared and her hair mussed. Sometimes when she got very upset, she would completely meltdown with stress. I'm only surprised that she wasn't even more of a mess, given the gravity of murder.

"You seem okay, at least." I said.

"You flatter me, Jon. I know I'm a mess." She replied in her usual kind way.

"You always look fine, anyway, milady." Miss Karras spoke from inside. I caught a glimpse of Miss Karras inside the room, shuffling her hands around in her handbag. "I was getting something from Susan's bag to calm her nerves. By accident, I knocked over a lamp." I craned my neck and saw a toppled table lamp on the carpet. It was unbroken, aside from the bulb. "Sorry about that."

"Not to worry. Has anyone mentioned to you what goes on?" I asked. Miss Jordain cocked her head, clearly in need of information. "James has taken the car to go into town and retrieve the police." I explained.

"In this weather!?" Miss Karras ran up to the door. Something looked off.

"You're concerned?" I asked.

"Of course I am! I've been in a car with him, it's a risk on a clear sunny day at the beach!" She pointed out. I stood in thought for a moment. I hadn't considered the fact that he had misplaced his own car just hours ago, despite it being mentioned numerous times.

"Ah." That was all I could think of to say. My pause was longer and more troubling than it should have been. "Well, all the same, just stay in your room until the storm subsides or the authorities arrive. Whichever comes first." I shrugged. "Staying in separate rooms will ensure that we all stay safe if the murderer is, indeed, still here."

"Do we know that everyone is here, though?" Miss Karras pointed out.

"How do you mean?" Miss Jordain voiced my own thoughts.

"We know about ourselves, but is everyone else accounted for?" Miss Karras specified. "Us and *all* the servants? Trust me, as one myself, I know you can't count them out." I perked up and turned.

"Mr Isaac!" I yelled out. I called loud enough for everyone to peek out of their rooms. Strangely enough, he was not at his post in the hall. It hadn't occurred to me when I ran out in a hurry. I prepared to call again when he came out of Lady Jilde's room at the landing. His first duty has always been to my aunt, so I couldn't be too cross that he was tending to her rather than watching the hall.

"Sir?" He stood to attention.

"Have you seen Mister or Missus Langley since dinner?" I asked. He thought for a moment then shook his head.

"Mrs Langley, I haven't seen since we served the dessert, but Mr Langley I haven't seen all day!" He said. I nodded and was about to speak when another crash of lightning lit up the manor in unison with a pounding on the front door! Mr Isaac and I looked at one another and both rushed downstairs! Everyone gathered up on the landing to oversee. More pounding echoed in the foyer, but before we could answer the door, Mr Isaac held me back. He gestured for me to wait and ran into the lounge. I was curious about what he was up to until he came back with a fire poker in hand.

"Good thinking." I whispered. More of the pounding came as I prepared to answer the door with Mr Isaac hiding just off to the side. I swung the door open and, with a gust of wind and rain, I made out two figures. Standing in the door-way was James! Bruised with a cut on his forehead, and aided by none other than Mr Wood!

"We have a problem!" Said Mr Wood. I lowered Mr Isaac's hand holding the poker.

"What's happened?" I asked as they entered the house.

"W-we're stuck..." James managed to groan.

Five

The entire Society was once again gathered in the lounge, this time in rapt attention to the two soaked and seemingly injured members. James was laid out on the couch getting some nursing attention to his brow from Miss Karras. Miss Cyrus was off, putting the raincoats in the laundry. When she returned she brought some blankets for James and Mr Wood. She wrapped Mr Wood first, which required aid from himself as he stood at almost over twice her height.

"Appreciated, Miss Cyrus." He stated. She, then, went over and began tucking a blanket around James, who was shivering.

"Roland?" Professor Cole tapped Mr Wood upon the arm and offered him a brandy. He accepted and proceeded to take one over to James.

"Don't you think he's had enough, Spencer?" Lady Jilde mused.

"I may not be a doctor of medicine, but I do know that this will help him to warm up." The professor shrugged.

"His constant consumption of alcohol was probably what gave him that gash on his forehead." My aunt continued.

"On the contrary, my lady." Mr Wood interjected, finishing another helping of his drink. "What gave him that gash was precisely what made me late."

"*S'il te plaît*, do explain." Mrs. Cole urged.

"Upon my arrival, shortly after the rain began, I started my approach up the hill, when I noticed a terrible ditch filled with tree limbs across the path. It was just past the hedge wall around your property." Mr Wood finished his drink and placed his glass on the mantle. "I narrowly stopped myself from driving directly into it, but at the cost of getting my vehicle trapped in soft mud."

"A ditch?" Lady Jilde seemed quite confused.

"We didn't see a ditch." Miss Jordain was also troubled by this information.

"We did see the gardener trimming limbs, though." Miss Karras added.

"Jonathan?" My aunt addressed me. "You said that Mr Langley was to trim the hedges today, not the trees." I nodded.

"It's true. And I find his lack of presence since earlier today highly suspect." I said. Mr Wood was very intrigued by the conversation. "Do continue, Mr Wood."

"Yes, as I was saying, I got out and attempted to remove my car from the mud, but if I had continued to try, I would have only succeeded in getting myself stuck as well." He said. "I thought that it would be far less the risk if I just scaled the pathway myself, enjoyed the party, and received help later. I had been stuck for approximately half an hour."

"Any way one puts it, you were going to be late." I said.

"The business that I was attending to ran a trifle over, but I *did* think I would make it in time." He added. "So, knowing that I had a fair walk ahead, I began pushing on against the growing storm. Luckily, I had a decent coat with me, but I do believe my shoes are shot. Anyway, I kept climbing away until I noticed some headlights coming my way. I couldn't be sure of who was on their way down, but I attempted to let the oncoming car know by waving them down."

"He didn't see you in the storm." The professor observed.

"Unfortunately, no." Mr Wood sighed. "And I had almost made it to the driveway. I hurried to follow the car back down the hill, but by the time I had caught up, it was already too late."

"Not going to lie," James spoke up. "I'm happy to know that the crash wasn't my doing alone." He chuckled.

"Indeed." The towering gentleman replied. "The remainder of the time we were both gone, I attempted to help James back up the hill to safety. And the rest would be where we are now." He finished.

"*Oui*, trapped in a house with no means of communication and a dead body in the dining room." Mr Wood sputtered at Mrs Cole's statement.

"I beg your pardon!?" He bellowed.

"Inspector Cormac is dead," I added. "He's been murdered."

"Poison, it would seem." James added, once again.

"My God." Mr Wood was stunned. "I don't believe it."

"Believe it, Roland. We've all been trapped in the estate with a cold-blooded murderer." Said Lady Jilde, shrugging haughtily.

"We still don't know it was anyone here, dear aunt." I specified. "We still have no accounting for the whereabouts of Mr Langley or his wife."

"The gardener?" Mr Wood asked.

"Indeed," I replied. "If I could find that man, I'd ask him a few questions about that ditch."

"*Tu veux dire*, you think that the gardener made the ditch?" Mrs Cole asked with a notion of impossibility.

"Well, we were the last to arrive." Miss Jordain pointed out. "After that point, it would not have taken long for him to make a mess of the main drive."

"The question is, how?" Mr Isaac joined in the conversation. "I'm not doubting that the timing could work, but it could only be done by a desperate man working for his life. Mr Langley has never appeared to be capable of a hard day's work if his life was under *threat*." The older man fought back a slight chuckle. Until today, Mr Langley's laziness was inconvenient, yet comical. But the situation was now dire.

"I think the better question is, why?" Chimed Miss Karras. "If he's so lazy, then he's got no gumption to hold grudges, so why kill the inspector?" What the young flapper said was true. I've seen men insult him and he shrugs it off, so what could Cormac have done?

"Firstly, I should like to take a look at things in the dining room." Mr Wood removed the blanket from his shoulders.

My aunt took another puff of her cigarette, clearly still under great stress and trying to hide it.

"Worried, *La demoiselle* Jilde?" Mrs Cole asked with strangely little comfort.

"Should we not, also, begin searching for the missing parties?" I suggested.

"We should, but we need more information." Mr Wood suggested. "And I do believe that splitting up would be foolish. There is no safety in numbers if someone with a weapon can pick us all off."

"I suppose that means I'd better get up." James sat up with a groan.

"You think you can?" Miss Karras asked as she and Miss Cyrus helped him to his feet.

"I think so. I've downsized to a small headache." He chuckled once more and waved the girls away to signify that he could walk by himself. We all crossed the foyer again and entered the dining room. Mr Wood looked down upon the body of Inspector Cormac. He didn't seem as taken with the horror that we were. He'd never said so, but I have always assumed that he had been in the Great War, so I doubt anything here comes close to horrifying him. He walked over and leaned down.

"What do we know?" He asked.

"Only that he died after dessert." Miss Jordain pointed out. Mr Wood stood up and looked at the table.

"Where is it?" He asked. We all looked at the table and noticed that it had been cleared! James and I were simultaneously the first to try running into the kitchen. What we found was Mrs Langley donning her raincoat!

"Mrs Langley!" I snapped, making her jolt. "What happened to the food?" I asked.

"Didn't want it to go wasting, did I?" She asked. "I put the last of the cakes into the icebox."

"Not all together I hope!" James ran over and opened the icebox to see the entire sheet of cakes on a tray. "Oh, no."

"Now don't go blaming my cooking for the Inspector keeling over." She said folding her arms. "I've never made anything sickly in my life."

"I don't think you did." Mr Wood stated, walking over to the icebox. He pulled out the sheet and set it on the counter. There were four full pieces and several partials inside of the tray making it impossible to tell which one had been Cormac's.

"Cinnamon almond." He said. He took a few whiffs over the top of the cakes. "This one in the corner smells a bit bitter."

"Cyanide." Miss Jordain whispered.

"Point to you, Susan." Mr Wood nodded. "An ingenious plan, poisoning someone by masking the scent with a matching food."

"Now wait a minute!" Mrs Langley called out. "I didn't do anything of the sort!"

"And you expect us to believe you?" Lady Jilde sneered.

"We should." Mr Wood suggested. "I don't think that she did this herself, after all, who else had access to the kitchen?"

"Well, everyone," I said. "Myself, James, Mr Isaac and Miss Cyrus had been in here today."

"But it was you, Mr Jonathan, that asked me to prepare the cinnamon almond cakes." Mrs Langley stated, once again, folding her arms.

"Because I like it!" I shrugged, not appreciating the sudden accusation. "We aren't even suspecting you."

"Oh? Then who is the first suspect if not me?"

"Your husband." Miss Karras stated, in a blunt tone. Miss Jordain grabbed her arm.

"Andrea." She scolded. "We can't throw out thoughts like that already."

"He dug a trap that's kept us here and now he's missing. You all may know fine literature on mysteries but I know people." The young maid defended her statement. "I'm not saying he *is* the murderer, but I am saying that he has some explaining to do." Mrs Langley seemed calmer already.

"Well, I haven't seen my worthless husband since this morning." She said. "He was most definitely acting strange, though."

"How so?" Asked Miss Karras.

"Bit fidgety, like." The cook described. "Very nervous, like the sword of Damocles was hanging over him."

"So something's spooked him." Miss Karras tapped her finger on her chin. "We still need to find him."

"In a storm like this, it'd be impossible for him to have left the grounds." I said.

"Then it might be all the more prudent for us to look for him in groups." The professor spoke up.

"Splitting off after all? A foolish suggestion for an academic." Lady Jilde scoffed.

"Even if it were one of us and not the gardener, we would hardly incriminate ourselves in confined quarters." Professor Cole explained to everyone. "We can move with those we surely trust."

"*Par example*, my husband and I will search in a pair and the rest shall choose your own groups." Mrs Cole added to her husband's point.

"Not a bad idea." I thought. "If I could make suggestions." Everyone awaited my instruction eagerly, urging me to continue. "I recommend James, Miss Jordain and Miss Karras to remain together, so as to keep the ladies safe. Myself, Mr Wood and Miss Cyrus will press on. The Coles, as suggested, along with Mrs Langley."

"And what of me, dear nephew?" Lady Jilde spoke down her nose. "You don't expect me to wander alone, do you?"

"Hardly. I wish for you to remain in your room, for safety with Mr Isaac on guard with his fire poker." Mr Isaac stood at attention again.

"My pleasure, sir." He said. "Milady?" He held out his

hand, Lady Jilde taking it, and began guiding her back to the staircase.

"As for the areas to search, I suggest the Coles take the cellar. James and the ladies take the second story. And the remaining of us will take the main floor." I further dictated. Miss Cyrus came to me as everyone dispersed to begin the search.

"Thank you for allowing me to come with you, Mr Jonathan." She said. "I'm not like Miss Karras, I don't have the confidence to defend myself in this situation."

"You won't have to worry. If the need should arise, I have the utmost belief that you'll defend yourself just fine." Mr Wood nodded to the young maid. I agreed and we set off into the house. We had to find Mr Langley before the storm let up and he could get away.

"Miss Cyrus?" I tapped her shoulder. "To begin with, is there anywhere here on the main floor that you haven't been, to your knowledge?"

"Uh, I haven't been to the laundry area besides leaving the coats inside." She stated. "I didn't even turn the light on, I simply left them on the drying rack within the light of the hall."

"I see." Turning myself toward the laundry room, which was directly beneath the upper landing. I opened the door, noticing the room was completely pitch black aside from the ray of light from the hall. I stepped in and reached around for the drawcord to ignite the single bulb overhead. The entire room was not especially large and was neatly organized, other than the wet coats hanging to the side of the door.

"Surprisingly empty." Mr Wood observed. "Even for only two people in this house."

"I believe Lady Jilde recently downsized her wardrobe." Miss Cyrus spoke up.

"Even more surprising." Mr Wood chuckled. "Well, there doesn't appear to be any place to hide here." The moment he said that something donned on me.

"Stupid!" I gave my forehead a considerable slap. "The first place we should be looking! The gardening house!"

"Yes, I've seen Mr Langley loaf about back there on many of my visits!" Mr Wood grabbed the damp coats from the rack and pressed one to me.

"What should I do?" Miss Cyrus asked.

"True, I don't feel comfortable leaving her alone." I said. "Her risk in the storm with us is less than staying in the house alone." Mr Wood immediately draped the coat around her and ran back to the foyer to retrieve the one he had come in.

"Just stay between me and Jonathan." He told Miss Cyrus. I lead the way around the corner to the French doors that open to the garden around the back. The patio on the opposite side of the doors was visibly damp but held some cover from the gazebo-style roof above it. The wind had cluttered the patio furniture to the side and the doors were rattling against the laws of nature. Beyond that was a wall of darkness and rainwater, even during the flashes of lightning. The gardens, as well as their caretaker's workhouse, were obscured by the heavy weather.

"When I open these doors, there will be a substantial gust to push us back. Try to lean into it and keep ahold of one another." I instructed. For safety, I fastened the latch on the bottom of the left door and prepared to open the right. "Ready?" Mr Wood took hold of Miss Cyrus's hand and she gripped the cuff of his coat, also doing the same with me as I took her other hand. The door nearly knocked me over as it was blown open with flecks of rain sputtering through. We pushed against the howling wind and I used what upper body strength I had to pull the door shut again.

Once it was latched we pressed on. We stayed in our human chain as we left the safety of the gazebo roof. Miss Cyrus lifted the oversized coat to make a hood for herself as her small frame would likely drown otherwise. Once in the rain, I could see the gardener's house in the flashes of lightning. Even with the storm, I knew the garden path like the back of my hand, and lead our trio to the large shed. Upon reaching the door I pushed and pulled, only to find it locked! Blast!

"It's locked!" I called out. Mr Wood stepped up, still gripping Miss Cyrus until he handed her off to me.

"Stand back!" He shouted over a clap of thunder. He put his entire body into a kick that broke the bar from the door and it swung free from its latch! We hurried in and closed the door again to keep the weather from following us in. With the latch broken it proved difficult to hold back the door.

"Mr Jonathan?" Miss Cyrus handed me a rake to bar the door, which I did, promptly.

"Thank you, my dear." I nodded. The three of us shook off our coats and looked around. The place was a complete mess. "My, my, it's no wonder he never gets much done."

"I dare say, it will be some difficulty for us to find any clues about him." Mr Wood said. "Least of all his whereabouts." He began looking over things atop the workbench.

"Something will stand out," I said in return. "Just look for something in place and orderly." Miss Cyrus chuckled. She walked over and used the sleeve of her coat to wipe the window while I joined Mr Wood.

"Well, the tools I saw him with earlier today are still missing." I observed the tool rack. As I had said, the tools he used for digging the trench and pruning the trees were missing from the rack.

"How can you tell?" Mr Wood laughed.

"Balance of probability. It may be cluttered in here, but I don't see the tools anywhere else-" I was, then, interrupted by Miss Cyrus.

"Beg your pardon, Mr Jonathan, but were they in a wheelbarrow?" She asked me.

"Indeed, they were." I stepped away from the tool rack to join her by the window. She pointed off to the side where an overturned wheelbarrow laid with tools strewn from it. "Interesting. Why did he leave the tools out?"

"I believe he was locked out of here himself." Mr Wood said. "There is a hammer missing from the table." He pointed at a hammer shape in the dust on the table along with some scuff marks. "And look." He gestured to the window on his side of the gardening house. There were nails in the frame on the outside! "It seems that someone barred Mr Langley from entering the gardening house after leaving."

"So, then, what does this mean?" Miss Cyrus asked.

"It means, we have some further questions for Mr Langley." I added. My eyes laid on something, suddenly, and I rushed to uncover it on the table.

"Jonathan?" Mr Wood queried. I reached under a canvas

tarp and pulled out a card, just like the ones I used in the game. I turned it over and it read, 'The Red Herring'. Turning it to my companions, they looked on it with the same bewilderment that I had.

"We need to find him." I said. "With this, I think we can conclude that he's in as much danger as we are."

"Could there be some tracks to follow out by the wheelbarrow?" Miss Cyrus asked, gawking back out of the window.

"That may be an idea." Mr Wood agreed.

"Here!" Before we took the rake from the door to leave, I took two torches from the shelf above the table we were searching and handed one to Mr Wood. "These might aid us in our tracking."

"Good thinking, Jonathan." He cheered. We lit the electric devices and took ahold of the small maid's arms once again. Mr Wood un-threaded the rake from the door, making it swing open from the wind. Miss Cyrus yelped a bit, as the door barely missed her face! She pulled the coat over her head again and we pressed on into the torrent. We crossed the front of the gardening house until we reached the overturned wheelbarrow. I knelt down next to it and shone my torch. There were some scrambled footprints in the shallow mud!

"Tracks!" I pointed out. I traced the light along the line of footprints, which seemed to head into the direction of the garage. "They go this way!" I waved them to follow me and we made our way toward the back door of the garage as quickly as we could. Thankfully, the wind died down a bit, but the rain remained the same.

Once we reached the door to the back of the garage, we noticed that it was ajar. I nudged it open and myself and Mr Wood shined our torches in. He gestured me to stay with Miss Cyrus as he entered, himself, first. He waved us in, indicating it was safe.

"Mr Langley?" He called. I traced my torch down at the muddy prints on the floor.

"Mr Wood." He turned and I pointed at a few drops of blood mixed in with the mud. Miss Cyrus started to gasp but I covered her mouth until we knew what was going on. Mr Wood and I moved our torches across the floor, tracing the muddy and bloody tracks. Our lights stopped at a mud-covered working boot. I slowly raised my light to a wet coverall leg and further still to a torso covered in blood! I raised it once more to see the stoic face of Mr Langley! Miss Cyrus screamed from behind my hand and I turned her away.

"Good lord..." Mr Wood placed his hand to his mouth, furrowing his dampened moustache. "This has become far more serious..."

Six

"Should we do anything?" Miss Cyrus asked Mr Wood and myself. Mr Wood arched over the body and sighed after checking him over.

"What can be done?" He said. "The man is dead, and in this storm, we can't move him."

"We should hurry back to the house and report our findings," I suggested. "But first, do you know how Mr Langley died?"

"He's been shot in the chest. I'd wager he came in through that back door after failing to enter his work shack and was shot." Mr Wood speculated. "He didn't die immediately, otherwise he'd have been on the ground by the door. He crawled over and expired from his wound." He tilted his head slightly and stroked the bottom of his beard. "Didn't you hear or see anything?" I walked over and took a knee next to the body as well. Upon laying eyes on the bullet wound, my mind was flooded with a terrifying revelation.

"When James and I were in here, readying the car, he

started the engine and the exhaust backfired." I explained. "But supposing, now, it wasn't a backfire that we heard!"

"Mr Jonathan, what are you saying?" Miss Cyrus shuddered.

"I think the murderer was in the garage *with* James and I!" I gasped. Mr Wood shot up and turned around.

"Back to the house!" He said, picking me up and pushing me toward Miss Cyrus. We took advantage of the lesser wind and ran back inside through the joining door that enters the kitchen. We slipped in and threw our coats down. Miss Cyrus instinctively went to pick them up, but I pulled her along and we re-entered the foyer once again.

"*Everyone!*" I called. "Come quickly! We've found Mr Langley!" As I expected, that brought everyone running, immediately. James and the ladies came from upstairs along with my aunt and Mr Isaac. The Coles and the cook did not come right away, however. Before I could think any further on that, Miss Jordain gave each of us a delicate looking over. Usually, she is the one requiring a mother's touch, but now she was mothering all of us.

"Are you all okay?" She asked. "You all look affright. Were you outside?"

"We were." Mr. Wood sighed. Miss Karras looked around.

"Where's the gardener? You said you found him, right?" She tilted her head.

"We did. Dead." I placed a finger to my chest. "He was shot." James looked at us, taken aback.

"How did we not hear a gunshot?" He queried. "That's not something that's very subtle."

"We did, James. When the car backfired." I suggested.

"You mean-?"

"Yes. The murderer was in the garage with us, watching us, and shot Mr Langley when he came in for shelter!" I explained. "And that's not all." I reached into my breast pocket and pulled out the card that we found. James leaned in and read it.

"*The Red Herring*? Isn't this one of the game cards?" He asked.

"Not one of the ones I put at the dinner table." Before I could speculate any further with the others, the professor and his wife came stumbling through the hall. They came running from the cellar area.

"Where were you two?" Miss Karras shrugged. She looked around them. "Oh, don't tell me."

"Mrs Langley vanished." Stated Professor Cole. "She slipped away while we were in the cellar." We all stood stunned, unable to decide between feelings of frustration or dread.

"You all have some issue with keeping an eye on people." Lady Jilde scoffed. Mrs Cole rolled her eyes, subtly, but I did notice.

"Did we hear you say you've found the gardener?" She asked us.

"They did, but he didn't answer any questions." James chimed in. Miss Jordain slapped his arm.

"Distasteful." She scolded him. He shrugged to indicate, as we all know very well, that tastefulness and tact are not his forte.

"He's dead." Mr Wood sighed. "Shot through the chest." I expected some form of French exclamation from the fine-suited woman, as per usual, but she stayed silent and looked to her husband and he to her. They looked concerned.

"Do excuse me." Professor Cole tried to excuse himself. "I

have to check on something." He was twiddling his decorative walking stick in his hands nervously.

"Where?" Lady Jilde spat.

"In my suitcase. I have to make sure something is safe." He replied as he climbed the stairs. Lady Jilde watched him from the landing and took another puff of her cigarette.

"A pair of something, more like." She chuckled. We were all too focused on the gravity of the situation to pay the comment any mind, but it seemed to rattle the Coles. The professor seemed especially confused but continued on his way.

I kept off to the side while the others discussed things, trying to avoid the eye line of the professor's wife. My aunt was too busy looking down on the mixed up conversation about the meaning of the card I had found. As I passed Mr Isaac, he glanced at me and I gestured for him to keep mum on where I was going. He nodded discretely and I slipped down the hall to find the professor. I found one of the doors ajar and peered in through the crack. I guided my gaze across the room, scanning toward the bed. The professor had his back to the door opening his suitcase that he'd retrieved from the car. I wouldn't read too much into it other than it may have had some sensitive information hidden between a spare shirt. It was possible, I supposed, that this could have all been set up to steal something of historical value. I continued to watch as he opened a secret compartment under the lid. He hunched over and dug around inside, pulling something out. If I didn't know the Coles better, the both of them, I'd swear it looked like a revolver! He seemed to breathe a sigh of relief and put the object away.

I moved away from the door as stealthily as I could. I rejoined my aunt and Mr Isaac at the landing. I joined in looking down on the others, myself, as they all conferred on theories. It seemed that they had moved on to the suspicious means of the gardener's death. They'd just finished discussing the odd trap at the gardening house. They all had the same school of thought that someone had barred the inside of the shed, exited through the window, and carefully nailed the window shut.

"And what were you checking on, dear nephew?" Lady Jilde asked, drawing my attention from the ongoing conversation.

"Nothing of much importance, aunt." I replied, trying to keep what I saw quiet so as not to upset her.

"That's not like you to follow something unimportant." She chuckled to herself. "All the same, I think you might do well to keep an eye on the Coles." I turned my attention to her.

"Do you know something, aunt?" I asked her. Mr Isaac looked to me along with Lady Jilde.

"Nothing of much importance, nephew." She mused. Ever

since the murder of Inspector Cormac, she has seemed defensive and cryptic for reasons unknown. Lady Jilde knew more than she let on and I intended to find out what it was. It was, admittedly, better off staying secret... Apologies, I seem to be letting on too much, myself. The professor stepped up beside me at the top of the stairs and I turned to him.

"Did you find what you were looking for?" I asked him as he started to descend the stairs. He spun and looked at me, notably nervous.

"Y-yes." He cleared his throat. "Yes I did, thank you."

"What was it?" I pressed. His left hand seemed to tremble. Something that I knew was a sign of him either lying or evading. Professor Cole was a terrible card player.

"Um, if you'll excuse me, I need to discuss something with my wife." He continued down the stairs. I pondered this and followed him down, looking back up at my aunt who retreated to her room with Mr Isaac in tow. Thinking back I wondered where Mr Isaac was when I ran into the hallway before when he was supposed to be outside her door standing guard. I described much earlier that the hall was empty and only at this point did it dawn on me.

"Assuming this theory is true, we still need to find out what's happened to Mrs Langley." James pointed out.

"Theory?" I asked. Unfortunately, rejoining the group was not so subtle, as I had no idea what the others discussed.

"Where were you?" My American friend asked me.

"I was checking on my aunt." I made sure not to betray my omission of checking on Professor Cole. *I* was a very good card player.

"Ah, I see." He sighed.

"We proposed the theory that this murderer seems to be perverting the game that you've set up into a trap to ensnare us." Mr Wood explained with a stroke of his beard. "Who else knew about your surprise game?"

"Only myself, Lady Jilde, Mr Isaac and you." I listed off. James looked at Mr Wood with a stern expression.

"You knew about this?" He waved his hand around.

"I visited several days ago. I noticed some slightly concealed things that, I had surmised, were meant to be clues for the game." Mr Wood pointed to one of the wall planters, walking over and pulling a very out of place envelope out. He glanced my way. "This was made to be a clue, yes?" I nodded. He opened the envelope and looked at the letter I had written. "It reads: 'For your next clue, search the pile of corpses that once stood tall and strong.'"

"The woodpile for the fireplaces?" Miss Jordain queried. I nodded once again.

"It was childishly easy, I know, but it was only the third clue of the game." I shrugged.

"I believe that whoever has sabotaged the game insists on us playing their deadly variant in order to find out who they are." Mr Wood explained.

"And where does Mrs Langley fit into all this?" Asked Miss Karras.

"Exactly why we must find her." I said. "Oh, this is beginning to get repetitive, isn't it?" Shaking my head, I looked over to the Coles. The professor seemed breathlessly distressed.

"Professor? Are you alright?" I asked as he balanced on his wife's shoulder, hand to mouth.

"The anxiety of th-*all* of this is getting to me, finally, is all." He stammered through the statement.

"*Viens mon amour*, sit." She led him into the lounge and sat him down on one of the chairs.

"Miss Cyrus, please look after these two," I ordered.

"We'll continue the search for the cook." I assured the couple. Before they could reply I rushed to James and grabbed him by the arm. "James, come with me." I urged.

"Wait, what about the ladies?" He shrugged.

"Mr Wood?" I called, keeping my voice down.

"I'll keep watch and we will look for your cook." He said. I dragged James upstairs, to his confusion.

"What's got into you?" He asked me, drifting along in my grip instead of fighting me.

"We are about to look in Professor Cole's suitcase." We entered the guest room and I pointed to the case, which was poorly hidden under the edge of the bed.

"Okay." James simply shrugged and knelt down next to the bed to retrieve the case. Upon placing it on the bed, we unlatched it and opened it. "So, what is it we're looking for?"

"Hang on a moment." I felt around the inside of the lid for a concealed latch. What I found was an elastic hook inside of the lid, which I pulled loose and lowered the hidden panel. Inside was only a bundle of lady's clothing and, um, *unmentionables*, for want of a tactful term.

"Surprising," James said, looking over my shoulder. "I

didn't take Amelia for the type. Especially such good taste in it." He mused. He pulled out a very fine lavender negligee, but before I could snap at him to stop messing with Mrs Cole's personal things, out tumbled a gun! A .45 revolver, black metal and a brown wooden grip.

"Even more surprising." I picked up the gun and opened the chamber to check the bullets within. I rotated it and sure enough, there was one missing. "*Neither* of them seem the type."

"It couldn't have been either of them, though. They were both inside when we were in the garage." James explained.

"Not quite." I paused. "If you recall, the professor went out to his car to retrieve this very suitcase."

"I just can't believe either of them could be responsible." James was more adamant about this than I'd ever seen him about anything in his life.

"Well, I trust you remember what Sherlock Holmes once said? '*When you eliminate the impossible, whatever remains, however improbable, must be the truth*'." I shrugged. "The most prudent thing would be to ask them about the meaning of this." I waved the gun, safely in a reverse position, don't worry. I put it into my smoking jacket and cinched it closed for us to go join the others and ask the professor and his wife a few questions. Or, we would have done, if we didn't run into Mrs Cole before we could even exit the room!

"*Qu'est-ce que c'est?* What are you doing in here?" She seemed outraged, which was a dangerous position for James and I to be in. When Mrs Cole was in an unfavourable mood, there was no telling what misfortunes might befall us. We were both about to speak, but she glanced behind us at the opened suitcase. She gasped and kicked the door shut! I would quote what she said here, but she started yelling at us in such frantic French that I couldn't catch a word of it.

"Amelia!" James tried to calm her down. "Slow down, neither of us can catch what you're saying!"

"How dare you go through my *husband's* personal items! I couldn't expect this from either one of you! I can't believe I have to go through this again!" She paced the entire room while ranting at us. She'd have kept going on, too, if I hadn't pulled out the gun that I found. As I assumed, she stopped in her tracks. She looked back and forth between me and the gun several times, stunned with nothing to say.

"I saw your husband with this earlier." I began explaining to her. "There's a bullet missing."

"He did *not* shoot your gardener." Mrs Cole stomped her foot.

"I wouldn't think so either, but he has a gun that's one shot shy." I gestured it to her. "I think this warrants some answers and I'm perfectly willing to listen."

"We just want a comprehensive reason for why he has it." James added. Mrs Cole sighed.

"Was that... all you found in there?" She asked us. Something had her perturbed and it seemed strange.

"Aside from your delicates." James blurted out. I smacked his head, silently begging for more tact and fewer reasons for Mrs Cole to use the gun on us!

"Mine? You don't-" Mrs Cole stopped herself before she overindulged us with information. I cocked my head and would have asked anything else if James hadn't chimed in with a shock.

"Oh, then those were your husband's?" James stated. "In some ways, that makes more sense." He seemed chipper about this, but Mrs Cole started to panic. "I say, Amelia, calm down."

"How could you have guessed that!?" She flew into a panic, her hands mussing her hair. It still had a shine, but now lacked its smooth comb-down, fluffing out with some volume. "*Stupide!* Why couldn't I keep quiet!"

"I guessed because I know people just like him from my nightly escapades. I've wondered quite often about him because of his looks and demeanour. I wondered about his '*preference*' for a while, but he clearly was in love with you, so I assumed your relationship was genuine." James continued, validating everything that I was still incredibly confused about. "I never thought it would be polite to ask." That was the breaking point of my silence.

"Really? For *that*, you care about politeness?" I flung my hand in the air, making the other two duck to avoid the gun in my hand. "Sorry." I lowered my hand sheepishly.

"This isn't like my usual kind of fun, this could be damaging to Spencer's reputation." James listed. "I only damage my own, already sullied, reputation. *That* is fun. Damaging others' I just find cruel." Hearing him say this made me realize something insightful about my close friend all of a sudden.

"I see," I said to him. "*That's* why you live the way you do." Mrs Cole also seemed to catch on to the subject as well.

"Your family is not shunning you, *you* are shunning *them*." She pointed to him. "They live in the circles you find cruel, like most well-off people, and you try your best to ruin them." She almost chuckled at the backward comedy of James's life.

"Plus, it's fun and I get paid for the pleasure." He gripped his collar like a proud politician.

"Can I count on your discretion, James?" Mrs Cole begged.

"Of course." He shrugged. Mrs Cole's plea got me back on track with the moment at hand.

"Yes, I still don't understand," I queried, needing to know. "Because, you have to admit, it is strange for a man to wear women's clothes." If looks could kill, the one I received from Mrs Cole would have erased me from the face of the Earth.

"It is *strange* for my husband to express himself in the comfort of our own home? Is it strange for him to be himself? *Est-ce étrange pour lui de savoir qui il est?* Is it his fault that the world's social convention would *ostracize* him for liking something outside of normal social dictation? Or that I think he looks *merveilleux!*" She took off her suit jacket and threw it at me. "And if his preference is discovered then his career would be *ruinée.*" She huffed, angrier with the world than us now. "And to top it all off, somehow it has already been found out and he's been *blackmailed* over it."

"*Blackmail!?*" James and I both hissed simultaneously.

"How has he taken it!?" James asked.

"He does not know. I've been paying it for months." Mrs Cole sat on the bed, but restlessly, got back up to pace again.

She was on the verge of tears, clearly wishing she had said nothing.

"Do you know who it is?" I asked. Suddenly, her sad demeanour changed back to anger.

"I do know. I've known for the last few weeks." She walked up to me. "Your aunt." James and I both stood, agape. I couldn't believe my ears, but another part of me knew full well that it was true. Actually, I knew it for a fact.

Seven

I was reeling from the revelation that my aunt was a blackmailer! And not only that, but she was blackmailing our *friends!* Lady Jilde had stooped to the crime of blackmail after all her pious talk that I had to sit through for my entire life. Thinking back, she has always been very contradictory in nature with a born-again belief, but an uppity and snobbish attitude. But this was too much! She was another example of those who just use religion for an image instead of an actual belief system. However, as I described before, I knew it had to be true. Above all, I knew why she was doing this, I just couldn't understand why she chose those closest to us!

"There has to be some kind of mistake." Said, James. "That bat is far too *holier-than-thou* for something like that. You've seen the way she treats me and all I do is drink obscenely and partake in multi-amorous evenings." He shrugged.

"*Oui,* but she probably does it because she finds what my husband does *répugnante* on a more prejudiced level." Mrs Cole huffed.

"I think it's very sweet that you're not repulsed by James's activities." He smiled.

"Oh, I am." Mrs Cole scoffed. "I just don't judge." James laughed and sighed.

"If I were to meet someone to settle down with, not very likely, but I would want them to be just like you." James patted her shoulder and tried to help her smooth her hair back down.

"There's no mistake, James." I pointed out, finally joining the conversation. "I'm sure that Mrs Cole is right."

"How do you figure?" He asked. I took a deep breath and released it because I was going to have to reveal something that my aunt wanted to keep secret. Quite ironic, come to think of it.

"Because the estate is failing." I blurted in a rushed statement. James and Mrs Cole both took a step back, thoroughly shocked by what they had heard.

"*Vous demander pardon?*" Mrs Cole snapped. It became my turn to pace the room. I couldn't believe I, so abruptly, revealed our own biggest secret.

"What happened?" James waved his hands at me. I shook my head and rubbed my temple.

"I'm not entirely sure. Bad investments? Just money running out? Whatever it may be, my aunt has not, outright, told me so." I began the sordid description. "I simply figured it out from several things. Downsizing her wardrobe, letting more of the help go, and even asking me to stay here with her. I knew things weren't well for a few years. But somehow she always managed to keep up with everything without having to give up the estate."

"And now you know how." James shrugged. Something occurred to me and I felt that it was necessary to look into it. I hung my head out of the door.

"Miss Cyrus!" I shouted down the hall toward the stairs. Caution was in the heavy, storm laden, winds and I didn't care about being covert at the moment. I tucked the gun away into my smoking jacket, nearly forgetting that I was still holding it. We all waited in the room for the prompt maid to come. We could hear her shoes tapping along the floor quickly until she reached the guest room we were all in.

"Yes, Mr Jonathan?" She panted. "What are you all doing in here?" She seemed confused, although her reason for being so was just.

"My aunt paid your salary already, yes?" I asked. She shuffled, thrown off by the oddly timed question as well as the complicated answer.

"Um, I think that is low on our list of concerns right now, is it not?" She fumbled around her words and twiddled her fingers. I knew she was hiding something.

"Does she pay you at all?" I asked in a firmer tone. It wasn't my intention to intimidate her, but I knew I was by towering over her with these questions. She looked at me, the others, and back to me with a contrite look. She shook her head in the depiction of '*no*'. "I see. It has recently come to my attention that my aunt supplements the estate's income by blackmailing. You don't have to if you don't want to, but can you tell me if she has something on you?" She shuffled once again where she stood.

"... I have family that has... been in prison..." She said. "My father was a robber and my mother was placed in prison for trying to conceal him."

"*Mon Dieu.*" Mrs Cole exclaimed. "You poor child."

"Child is very correct. I was eleven when I lost my parents." Her voice cracked, indicating that she was going to start crying. James reached for a handkerchief to give her, but as it wasn't his suit, he forgot he didn't have one. I reached into my smoking jacket, narrowly avoiding the pistol, and gave her one of my own. "Thank you." Miss Cyrus took it and dried her eyes. "I used to live in London but, with a thief in the family, no one would hire me to do anything." She sniffled. "I left the city and came to Oxford, hoping to find something decent that didn't involve dying young in a work-house."

"I see." James chimed in. "But instead of finding something that pays, you found fruitless slavery."

"It didn't start that way. I was being paid and saving was easy since I live in the servant quarters." She said. "But last year, Lady Jilde asked me into her room where she discussed what she had found out about me and I begged her not to dismiss me." A sob escaped her throat.

"And she didn't." I speculated. "How did she find out?"

"I don't know, but even though I was being kept as free labour, I viewed it as better than the alternative. I still have a place to live, food, clothing and I have managed to learn so much listening in on the Society's book meetings." She relaxed a moment but another sob burst from inside her chest. "But I still keep thinking about how I can't escape my past. She pleases herself by reminding me of it whenever the fancy strikes her."

The three of us, I could tell, were trying to think of something to make her feel better. I could only think of one thing that I wanted to do at this moment. I stormed out of the room and into the hall, making my way to the staircase and descending it so fast it looked like I was flying down ethereally! I rounded the corner into the lounge and gave the room a scan.

Everyone was still here apart from the few who had come upstairs and were now running down to catch up with me.

"Everyone?" I tried to keep my voice down so as not to alert Lady Jilde to my conversation but my body language betrayed my stress.

"Are you alright, Jonathan?" Miss Jordain came up to me and rested her hand on my shoulder. "You look like you've found... another body?"

"No, but I think there may be another one before the night is out if we're not careful." I said as the other three followed me in. "Some new information has come to light and I feel compelled to ask the rest of you if you know anything about it."

"And what might that be?" Miss Karras asked, scanning me up and down for some reason.

"Have any of you been blackmailed by my aunt?" I cut straight to it, tired of beating around the bush. The entire room was as silent as the guest room was when Mrs Cole told us about her situation.

"That's not a very funny joke, Jonathan." Said Mr Wood, stoic as a statue.

"It's no joke, Mr Wood." Miss Cyrus spoke up. "My employment here is based on blackmail."

"And myself." Mrs Cole brushed her forehead and leaned against the archway. Professor Cole sprung to his feet from the couch, shocked.

"*Excuse me!?*" He shouted. "How? When!?"

"Lady Jilde!?" Mr Wood was just as taken, as he had known my aunt longer than my late uncle! "Why? She fancies herself so high-held, why would she stoop to the most boorish crime in the book?"

"I believe she does it because she sees herself so '*high held*'." Miss Jordain chimed in. "She's been blackmailing me, too." Her expression sank from anxiety to depression.

"What!? What the hell do you mean she's been blackmailing you!?" Miss Karras shrugged in a frenzied fashion.

"That *and* the estate is losing money, so she seems to be supplementing the income by blackmailing those she deems..." James paused. "What was it, Amelia? *Répugnante.*" She nodded. He smiled, proud of pronouncing the statement correctly, but it was very inappropriate for the moment at hand. What else is new for him? Mr Wood had to sit on the arm of the couch, taken off guard by the new information.

"I know how you feel, Mr Wood. I was surprised exactly the same way." I reassured my mentor.

"Take a step back!" Miss Karras shouted. "How long has that festering hag, sorry Jon, been taking money from you!?" She stamped her heeled foot.

"Two months ago." Miss Jordain hung her head with her arms crossed. "She and I had gotten into a disagreement and said if we tried to leave she would reveal our... *my* secret. But it wasn't so much that I couldn't explain away the extra expense to my family, so I didn't think it was worth worrying you about it."

"'*Wasn't worth worrying me about it*?'" Miss Karras turned defensive. "Anything that happens to you is my concern! It's literally my job!"

"But it doesn't mean I have to force more burdens on you."

"You're so fragile, though. I'm here so that your burdens can be shared." Miss Karras sat down where the Professor once sat. Miss Jordain walked over and sat next to her.

"I understand that you're here for me, but I deserve to be there for you from time to time as well." She said to her friend. Miss Karras nodded and smiled.

"Well, that being said, Jon was right. There may be a new body tonight!" Miss Karras bolted to her feet and started to stomp toward the foyer. She was cracking her knuckles like some bare-knuckle brawler but I took her by the shoulders and held her back. "Jon, don't stop me!"

"Hold on, Miss Kar-"

"*Andrea!* Is it so hard to just say our names!? We've been friends for years, we've danced, we've drunk together, we've sat and discussed books together! Just call me by my name!" She stomped on my foot with her heel and I fell over with an exclamation of pain. "Oh, Jonny, I'm sorry!"

"It's fine, I was just going to tell you to let me have it out with my aunt." I managed to get back to my, now aching, feet with James's help. I winced and regained my balance. "She'll likely be much more receptive to me interrogating her because it will catch her off guard to have me, of all people, openly cross with her." She was going to say more, but I held up my hand and limped back to the foyer and up the stairs with determination. I think I hid it well, but on the inside, I was seething. My aunt was guilty of a petty and disgusting crime to pad her purse and make herself feel higher than the only people close to her.

Before I knew it, I was at her door and pounding my fist against it. It was an out of body experience like I was watching it happen from down the hall. I looked over my shoulder to make sure none of the others followed me up. I could faintly see down to the bottom of the staircase, where I saw

Mr Wood keeping the others downstairs. I grew tired of waiting and forced the door open.

"Aunt!" When I entered the room, I felt nothing but instant regret. I staggered at the sight of Lady Jilde and Mr Isaac embraced in a passionate kiss! I would have had nothing to say, but I had come in, prepared to yell at my aunt, and in my astonishment, I let out a horrid screeching sound... I had never made such a sound before, and hopefully never will again.

"*Nephew!*" Lady Jilde shouted. Other shouting was coming from downstairs, but I was not paying any attention to them and just slammed the door shut.

"What the hell is happening!?" I threw myself against the door trying to erase the image from my mind. "Murder, mayhem and now this!?"

"Master Jonathan, I believe-" Mr Isaac began. I threw up my hands with an expression that could make him the next dead body.

"Given everything I've gone through tonight, I still need to process this moment, Mr Isaac." I growled. "How many more secrets are in this house? I've only just found out that this place has been financed by our only supportive friends by less than legal methods!"

"Oh?" My aunt looked at me arrogantly. "If I'm being perfectly frank, dear nephew, it's thanks to you that I thought of how to use their information for the betterment of all." She shrugged.

"*The betterment of all*? You're extorting the only people who take us seriously!" I yelled. "I'm surprised at you for being so '*sinful*', as you would put it! Not to mention carrying on with our butler!"

"People who live in glass houses, Jonathan." Lady Jilde grinned. "I may be committing a dishonest act, but some of them are far worse off than me."

"How do you mean? I can't understand your twisted thought process on this! What could they have done to warrant *this* much animosity from you!?"

"They're all an affront to civilized society." She sat in her vanity chair against the far wall. "The only ones I couldn't do anything to were Roland, who has never done anything. And James, who couldn't care less who knows of his... *debauchery*."

"What makes you think it's your place to take any action over what they do with their personal lives?" I tried to speak calmly, but I couldn't help but shake with anger. "Who are they hurting? Mrs Cole was paying you to protect her husband from being persecuted for wearing clothes outside of social dictation in the privacy of his own home."

"If he is doing nothing wrong, then why does he need protecting?" Lady Jilde grinned again, taking a puff from her cigarette holder. "Why would the university relieve him of his position if he did nothing wrong, *hm?*"

"That is the fault of a judgmental society that calls itself *'civilized'*. Meanwhile, the same people are the first to turn into evil, petty, animals to tear apart whoever is not conforming to their views." I tapped my foot and realized that I could come back at my aunt at her own game! "Doesn't your precious book tell us not to be conformed to this world? Romans 12:2, I believe?"

"You know another saying in the good book, dear nephew? That woman is not to be lain with woman." Lady Jilde sneered. "Atheistic, though you may be, you cannot deny the written statement in mankind's original belief system."

"Wha-?" I wasn't entirely sure where she was going with that statement until I realized that *that* was what she had on Miss Jordain and Miss Karras! They weren't just maid and mistress, nor were they just best friends. They were lovers! "Oh, I see. That's what you found on the Susan and Andrea." It also explained what made that lamp break in their room. I could have struck my own head for not putting it together sooner.

"So familiar all of a sudden, Jonathan. What's changed?"

Lady Jilde chuckled as though it were a novelty for me to care about my friends!

"You do realize that the evolution of the English language makes that statement very different, yes? '*Lain*', back in those days, directly references having... *relations*." I may not be a puritan, but this kind of conversation is still, to me, sensitive and awkward. "Doesn't the Bible *tell* us to love!? If you follow only the words and not the meaning, then your special manual is only instruction on how to hurt! You may believe in God, dear aunt, but if I understand the meaning of Matthew 7:23, God does *not* believe in you." I panted after my tirade and huffed. "It's a sad day when an atheist has better morals and understanding than someone like you."

"Whatever opinion you have on the matter, do you honestly think that those two *creatures* are not '*having relations*'?" Lady Jilde would not back down, and Mr Isaac remained off to the side, standing at his usual attention. He was staying out of the conversation, lest I lose my temper again and throw him out into the storm. I would have argued that what the ladies did with one another in no way affects her, but that would have just been beating a dead horse. Instead, another question came to mind.

"What did you have on Inspector Cormac?" I asked, turning the conversation on its ear to throw her off. It seemed to work, as she nearly dropped ashes onto the carpet.

"Mr Isaac? Would you care to explain? After all, it was you who brought the information to me." Lady Jilde put out her cigarette in the ashtray on the vanity. I turned to the nervous old butler. Sweat began beading on his temple.

"Inspector Cormac was not, in fact, with the police department." He said. Lady Jilde played this well. She knew I was trying to stun her and gave me something to stun me back! It worked.

"... I beg your pardon?" I had paused, trying to take that in.

"His credentials were false. He was a crude man who thought that feigning being a police inspector would help him climb the social rungs. To make his plan work he began associating himself with the members of the Criminology Society." Mr Isaac continued to explain to me. "In reality, he was a simple con man who made his living by stealing the livelihood of others out from under them with charm and a silver tongue."

"... I see." I felt so stupid... This was the reason I never had a liking for him. He was a fraud, and on some level, I knew it. "This makes much more sense. It also explains why he accepted Miss Jordain's donation to the constabulary a year prior."

"And why nothing changed for the police department after the donation was made." Lady Jilde said with confidence.

"So, do you still think my extracurricular activities serve no purpose?"

"I hope you don't think that this information in any way changes my mind about your conduct in this situation." I looked between my two elders. "Although, I would like a trifle more information on how *this* whole thing began." I pointed between them. They both went silent and Lady Jilde finally seemed a bit uncomfortable, which I took as a success. "Not so confident now, are you?"

"I fail to see why I have to justify my actions to you, nephew." Lady Jilde turned in her chair, looking into the vanity to adjust her makeup.

"Ah, see now, that's the issue right there." I tapped my chin. "You have no reason to justify your actions of carrying on with the butler, a complete degradation in high society, to others besides yourself. Now *why*, pray tell, does that sound so familiar?" Lady Jilde's expression to the mirror was one I could never put a price on. It was a swirling mix of anger, realization, worry and fear. "And you, with nothing to pay me with."

"Master Jonathan, please." Mr Isaac tried to have me back down.

"Although, I suppose an arrangement we could make would be for you to give up whatever information you have on the others." I shrugged. She whipped around and looked right at me.

"And what do we do about our home? Our lives!?" She spat. "We could lose everything. You are fresh from university and haven't even chosen a career for yourself, yet."

"Why didn't you ask Mr Wood for help? You know good and well that he would have helped! And do *not* go into any pride nonsense, because you know what your precious book says about *that!*" I stomped toward her by two steps, finishing the conversation. She was stunned by my brazen approach.

"I know we haven't always seen eye to eye, nephew, but I'm quite surprised at you." Lady Jilde's voice broke. She was clutching her chest in exaggerated fear.

"One day, aunt, everything you've done is going to catch up to you and there will be no one to turn to for help." I began to turn to leave.

"She would still have me, Master Jonathan." Mr Isaac tried to point out.

"And how is that?" I refused to even meet his gaze and remained oriented toward the door. "What means of support do you have besides service? You think my aunt, with all her selfish ways, would continue to love you in the face of poverty?" A strained silence filled the room enough to muffle the storm outside.

"I kept her safe this evening." Mr Isaac was fidgeting as he spoke with forced confidence.

"Standing by the door with a fire poker and then abandoning your post to kiss the mistress of the house?" My tone was flat.

"Mr Cormac had been blackmailed and I had reason to believe that he intended to kill Lady Jilde." I paused after Mr Isaac said what he did. "I had heard several conversations between him and Lady Jilde that turned to threats."

"Mr Isaac... " I spoke slowly. "How exactly did you keep my aunt safe?"

"... I murdered him first." He stated. Lady Jilde seemed unshaken by the fact. I stood in front of the butler, my mouth agape. I couldn't figure out what to say about that. "I thought it would be as simple as poisoning him with his cake. But things became more... complicated with the storm."

"... Uh... I don't..." I tried to process further with my arms still crossed. "How do you expect me to respond to *that!?*" I screamed. "Am I expected to *thank* you for it!?"

"I had to do something!" Mr Isaac defended his actions. "If

I didn't, then your aunt could be the one lying dead in one of these rooms!"

"So what happened to the poison you used? Where did you even get it?" I asked.

"I bought some earlier this week from the pharmacist under the pretences that we had a pest problem." He explained. "I put a few drops in Cormac's cake and in the confusion I tried to make my way to get rid of the remainder." He scratched the back of his head. "The thing that stopped me was everyone planning on calling the authorities. I had to hurry and disconnect the phone lines."

"You did that instead of attempting to call the police." I added, pinching the bridge of my nose.

"I had to slip away while everyone was in their rooms to pour out the last of the poison." Mr Isaac sighed, pulling out an empty vial from his cutaway coat.

"I let him pour it out in my washroom." Said Lady Jilde, resting her chin on the back of her hand. She still faced the vanity, not facing us. I'm sure a psychology expert would have an opinion.

"And what was the reason for killing Mr Langley, pray tell?" I spat back. He seemed stunned while my aunt continued to adjust herself in the vanity mirror, barely attentive to the conversation.

"I'm not the one who killed the gardener." He said. "With his wife missing, I had assumed that she had killed him." I threw up my hands once again.

"I'm going back down so that we can all find Mrs Langley and put an end to the chaos of this evening!" I put out my hand to Mr Isaac. "Give me the key."

"Whatever for!?" Lady Jilde finally turned to face me.

"Because I am locking this door until we get the authorities here," I spoke very firmly. "You will both have much to answer for after this."

"You can't just-" My aunt began to fuss, but Mr Isaac spoke up over her.

"I will take whatever punishment I must, but please, let Lady Jilde go free." He pleaded to me as he handed over the key.

"That all depends on the others." I said. "Forget the blackmail and they may as well. But I can neither promise they'll be as forgiving, nor that they'll simply let it go." I turned my back on them to head to the door.

I would have left them there but I was knocked off my feet by the door swinging open and dropping me to the floor! Before I came back to my senses, the sound of gunshots echoed throughout the house! I shook off my stunned daze and looked up at Lady Jilde, laying back in her vanity seat, with three bullet wounds!

"*NO!*" Mr Isaac roared and charged into the hallway. What happened made me feel like I was looking at it from the outside once again. I just witnessed a murder for myself and it was the murder of Lady Jilde! I looked over where Mr Isaac once stood and noticed that he had left the fire poker, that he had armed himself with, behind! The very next thing I heard as a climbed to my feet was another gunshot and a woman's scream! I couldn't focus on any one thing because there was so much happening at the moment!

"What the blazes!?" I heard more screaming from downstairs and the cries of distress from Miss Jordain. Looking down the bannister, I saw the Society gathered around the crumpled body of Mrs Langley with a revolver in her hand.

"Jonathan... " I turned around and saw Mr Isaac against the wall with his hand over his side. The final shot that happened in the hallway had gotten the old man!

Eight

I dropped to my knees next to Mr Isaac. He had been shot. Even without his advanced age, he wasn't likely to survive this. He winced as he covered his wound with his glossy crimson-covered hand. I wasn't sure what to do.

"Mr Isaac, I'm so sorry." I stated, almost numb to the situation.

"It's fine, Jonathan... I have to tell you something... " He wheezed. "This estate was never in jeopardy... I could have saved it."

"What do you mean?" I asked.

"Your aunt came into this estate after your late uncle passed away many years ago before you were even born... As far as your aunt ever knew, it had belonged to a friend of her husband's... I was that friend... " I had nothing to say to this. Not because I was shocked by the information, but because I didn't know how to take it! It was as though I just learned something as equally and oppositely shocking as the blackmail. "That look on your face is a laugh... " He chuckled.

"This place was yours? For longer than I've even been alive?" I brushed my hand through my hair.

"Indeed... I never wanted you or your aunt to know... I never even wanted to be an aristocrat... I just wanted a peaceful life without that... So I became the caretaker of the estate instead... " He began coughing in pain as blood began filling his lung. "But if the estate had truly fallen through, I would have saved it with my own fortune... I've never used it... I never had children, but knowing you all these years... I want it to fall to you... "

"Me? You're leaving everything to *me*?" I shook my head to aid my thoughts to catch up with me.

"Yes... Just don't squander or misuse it... " He smiled and I leaned in to whisper something to him.

"Goodbye, old man." I have to say I will never forget the look on his face for as long as I live. It was the fear of a man in his last vestige of mortality. He finally passed and I had lost him. My head hung low and I shed a tear for my fallen friend. If only there had been less anger in our last moments together, but at least we made amends in the very end...

I felt a hand on my shoulder and looked up to see Mr Wood. I believe he was there for most of the conversation but held back so as not to interrupt the moment. We both knew he would not survive the gunshot. We looked back into the bedroom of my aunt and Mr Wood put his hand to his mouth.

"My God... " He brushed his hand down his beard. "I'm so sorry, Jonathan. In the course of one night, you have lost *both* of your surrogate parental figures."

"I can't even tell if the shock has set in." I looked down at my hands. "How much of our conversation did you hear?"

"All but what you whispered to him." He replied. He pulled me in and hugged me tight like a father figure would to console their child. "We are all here for you, Jonathan. Let's head downstairs."

"Let's." I sighed and descended the stairs while Mr Wood hung back for reasons I can only assume were to say goodbye to my aunt. Everyone looked my way, Susan and Andrea running to me, embracing me, relieved that I was okay.

"Jonathan! I was so terrified!" Miss Jordain cried.

"We're glad you're alright." Miss Karras agreed. I looked over at James, who was examining the gun that was in Mrs Langley's hand.

"I think we found our overall murder weapon." He said, unfolding the handkerchief that he was holding the weapon with. "Given all of the shots we've had tonight, there is only one bullet left in the chamber. This is, without a doubt, the murder weapon." He looked down at the cook's soaked body. "Shame. I really liked your cook."

"I noticed." I rolled my eyes, slightly.

"*Cela pourrait-il signifier* Mrs. Langley was the killer?" Mrs Cole shrugged. "She had the means to poison dinner as well as clearly having access to the gun." She said pointing to the pistol.

"But, darling, what would the motive be to kill the inspector?" Her husband pointed out.

"To keep the police off of her trail until she could get away?" James asked.

"Well, if that were the case... " I looked up at Mr Wood, descending the staircase. "She killed Cormac for no reason at all. According to my aunt, who was blackmailing him as well, Cormac was a fake. He impersonated a police officer to get close to us as a social climber."

"Y'know, I never pegged him as intelligent enough to be a policeman." James chuckled. "If you think about it, he was pretty obvious."

"You refer to the fact that he usually agreed with our theories or finagled the conversations in lieu of coming to his own conclusions." Mr Wood added to James's point.

"Yes, indeed." James slicked back his black hair. "Not that I'm diminishing the tragedy of his death, you understand." Sliding his hands down to the collar of his jacket.

"We heard numerous shots." Professor Cole stated. "What happened up there?"

"Mrs Langley. She burst in and shot my aunt." I rubbed my eyes with a shaky sigh. "The silver lining I can assure you all of is that I believe all your secrets are safe."

"How can you be sure?" Miss Cyrus asked.

"My aunt was never much of a collector, outside of her favourite clothes," I explained. "Did she ever show any of you any proof of her knowing your secrets?" Everyone looked at one another and thought deeply. All my aunt told anyone was that she knew what their secrets were, but did not show that she could prove it to anyone else. With her gone, then everyone should be safe. "You see?"

"Then, are we free?" Miss Jordain gasped in emotional relief.

"Yes, Susan, you are. Both you *and* Andrea." I gave a weak smile. I turned to Mrs Cole and placed a hand on her shoulder. "After this blows over, I'll go through my aunt's belongings to make sure you are all free from your burdens." I glanced to the professor and back. She smiled and went over to her husband to hold him close.

"What now?" James asked. Everyone looked at him, perturbed. "What I mean is, does this mean the murder evening is over? This is clearly the gun used to kill her husband, but-"

"Well, did she seem like she was very loving toward her husband while you two were philandering in the kitchen?" I asked, eyebrow raised.

"She seemed to care enough about him to try and find him alongside us." James added.

"I suppose we'll never learn the true answer as to why that was." Said Mr Wood. We were all still so taken with the events of the evening. I walked over to the front door to take a glance out the window. The storm was still heavy, but not a veritable hurricane any longer.

"She may not have been the only one with a motive to kill Lady Jilde, but I doubt very much that she was the one to kill her husband." I pointed out. "When we saw her after we came inside from the garage, she was dry as a bone. Look at her now." I gestured at Mrs Langley's damp body.

"It's true." Miss Karras knelt down. She ran her hand against the fabric of the cook's coat and shook the excess water from her fingertips. "She's been outside within the last few minutes."

"Maybe she went to look for her husband's remains." The professor leaned on his walking stick. "It would account for her whereabouts when she disappeared."

"But the only remaining question is, where did she get the gun?" I asked. I pulled out the pistol I had taken from the professor's case. "I thought I had found it when I saw the professor pull this from the secret compartment in his suitcase." Professor Cole seized up and hyperventilated until his wife took his hand. "I'm not interested in anything in there besides *this*, Spencer."

"Ok-kay." He took a deep breath and sighed with his hand placed on his chest. "I was given that by a colleague on my last expedition when we had trouble with some marauders. They attacked our camp but I never used it. Never thought I would need to. But when everything began tonight, I wanted to retrieve something to protect my wife and me."

"The contents were both risky and *risqué*." James interjected. "Why bring the whole case and not only the gun in your coat?"

"Well, I tried." The professor slumped his shoulders. "I couldn't find it in the storm and then I, uh... got stuck head first." His sandy blonde hair hung over his face as he lowered his head in embarrassment.

"Ah, *then* you brought the whole thing in with you." James stifled a chuckle.

"When I followed you upstairs, I saw you look at it and put it back." I explained. Professor Cole perked back up, keeping balance with his walking stick.

"Yes! You had said the gardener was shot, so I went up to check that my gun was still there. I was entirely relieved that it was." He said, patting his chest.

"But if it was never used, why is there a bullet missing?" I asked Cole.

"Hm?" The professor tilted his head. "There isn't. I checked the chamber." I opened the chamber myself and showed the one empty slot. "But... But that's impossible! My revolver was never fired!"

"I believe you," I said. "And I also believe that the puppeteer behind tonight's events may be behind this little red herring as well." I clicked the chamber closed and handed the gun back to Professor Cole. He held it awkwardly, wanting very much to avoid gripping the trigger. "If I am right, then we aren't out of the woods just yet."

"You believe the mastermind is still in the house. Hiding away." Mr Wood nodded, understanding the suggestion.

"But how can they still be hiding from our gaze when we've been all over this house?" Miss Cyrus asked, clutching her apron.

"Oh!" Miss Jordain exclaimed. "I might have an idea! Far fetched though it could be." The entire foyer was in rapt attention to the lovely lady in white. "Many old mansion houses, when they were first designed, have been known to have secret rooms or passages. Even my parents' home had a secret area behind one of the bookshelves that I used to use as a playroom when I was a child."

"Far fetched, but not impossible." I ran my thumb along my jawline. I could feel the stubble that had begun to grow during the course of this extended evening. "My aunt lived here for a long time, but not since its beginning. According to Mr Isaac, he was the original owner, but he is beyond telling us the secrets of the manor."

"Indeed. He, too, is dead." Mr Wood hung his head.

"Oh, my, no!" Miss Jordain stepped back into Miss Karras's arms.

"Indeed. Mrs Langley shot him in the struggle upstairs." I said, solemnly.

"I hate to push mournful feelings aside, but, do you have any idea where this *'secret door'* might be?" James shrugged along with a cock of his eyebrow.

"I may be the one who's lived here, but I think this one is in Susan's wheelhouse." I gestured to the shy woman.

"You think *I* should lead this search?" She asked.

"Why not?" Mr Wood stepped to my side, resting a hand on my shoulder. "After all, this idea was posed by you. I would say that you may be our resident expert on secret doors." He chuckled. She nodded and was filled with precarious confidence.

"I'll do my best. But if this one rests on my shoulders, I would recommend that we all stick together this time, as opposed to splitting up." She explained, holding Andrea's arm.

"Safety in numbers." James nodded. "I like the idea." The entire group agreed.

"Very good." Susan clapped her hands. "Now, in the case of secret doors, I would say that we should seek the usual places that some of our favourite books show. They appear in areas such as bookcases and fireplaces. Other spots may include, behind tapestries or large paintings. But even a simple hollow point behind a wall can lead to a room."

"Well, there are no tapestries here." I laughed, amused at the idea. "But there are portraits and bookshelves in enough places to look around."

"Any ideas on where to begin?" James pointed in opposing directions.

"I would begin in the hallways." Mr Wood looked down the hallway. "Could there be anything in the back rooms?"

"Perhaps so." I led the way to the back and passed the French doors to the patio. I ran my hand along the opposite wall until I reached the door to the servant quarters. There was still one more room next to this one and the cellar, but we would check it after this. "Miss Cyrus? Would you mind if I enter?"

"Please do." The young maid said with a slight bow.

"That's unnecessary." I waved off the gesture. "Just because I'm the sole master of the house, doesn't mean you have to treat me differently." I opened the door to find the modest living conditions of Miss Cyrus inside. It wasn't as though the room was a dilapidated shack, as it was well kept inside, and it was very open but with few comforts. There was a bed with sheets, a stand by the head of it, and a wardrobe that looked as though it might have room for two outfits. Another table sat in the corner, nearest the door, with a simple washbasin and a mirror hanging above it. I hadn't seen this room in a long time and was shocked. To think that this room once held five people before my aunt dismissed the rest of the staff.

"Wow, Essie," James exclaimed. "You clean up very well for someone who lives like Cinderella."

"If I do take up ownership of this estate, this is going to change." I gestured.

"I get by well enough, Mr Jonathan." Miss Cyrus placed a hand on my arm.

"Getting by is one thing, living is another." I said, patting her hand. "If we don't make time to do something worthwhile, then why are we here?" She looked up at me. "I promise, when we make it through this, you will have a well-paid position and a life beyond the drudgery of work." She smiled with a glisten in her eye. "I'm not letting anyone else die tonight. We have ample surface area to search here, everyone fan out and begin knocking." The others did just that and spread along the four walls. We looked and listened for hollow points or triggers that could possibly open a door.

"Professor?" Miss Jordain pondered. He looked over his shoulder while tapping the lower wall with his knuckle and readjusting his glasses with his free hand. "You've been in tombs before, yes?"

"No, no." He chuckled. "But I see where you're going with

this. I *have* been in old places with secret rooms before. In fact, finding some sculptures and architecture behind a secret panel is what led me to meet Amelia." He looked at her longingly and his wife back at him.

"I think what she means is, do you know how someone could find out about a secret room without finding it?" Andrea added.

"Oh, well it *is* plausible if it is listed on an original floor plan, but someone would have to have that in order to find it." Cole explained. "The mastermind could be one of the old builders or someone who knew and had a grudge on the owner." He shrugged.

I continued listening to the others spin their theories, but something was irking me. Something was missing. Or should I say, someone? As I scanned the room I saw everyone except for Mr Wood. I elected not to alert the others as they continued their discussion, while I slipped out of the room. I looked up and down the hallway and stepped over to the closed door at the end of the hall. It was the door to the cellar and I couldn't think of a reason for Mr Wood to go down there... but I *could* think of something that was worth him going upstairs. I slipped by the servant quarters and around to the base of the stairs. I could tell there was movement going on up there and ascended carefully. The dim hallway was illuminated by another flash of lightning, the red hues from Mr Isaac's body glistening at the moment. I peered into my aunt's room, curious as to whether he might be in the room to examine Lady Jilde's body or to mourne. He wasn't in the room but I did notice something in the corner of my eye. I could see a light on in the hallway. It was the lamp from my own bedroom. I walked up to the slightly cracked door. The *Déjà vu* I was experiencing was almost laughable if not for the suspicious means of the events.

"Mr Wood?" I took a chance at calling into the room. I entered and found my room empty, except for one major difference. I looked directly at an opening that had to be what made Mr Wood come up here. There was, indeed, a secret panel... behind my writing desk! A hidden nook that slid to the side, thereby hiding my washroom door. Inside the nook was a series of pictures and notes, tied together. They depicted everything from the murder of Cassius Cormac, to the events happening at this very moment. This was all layered over a plan for my original party, pinned to the mansion's blueprints! Professor Cole was right about the plans showing every secret hideaway. The problem was, going by the notes on the board, things at this moment were apparently going off-script. The web showed that we were meant to conclude in the foyer. After which the killer planned to escape by locking the door to the lounge and escaping via a hidden tunnel behind the fireplace!

"Jonathan." I heard Mr Wood's cold voice behind me. I turned quickly, nearly losing my balance as I caught myself on the writing desk. "Are you surprised at *this* conclusion?" I looked between him and the wall.

"I'd be lying if I said I wasn't." I replied.

"As the old adage goes, '*the best-laid plans often go awry*'." Mr Wood held his hands firmly at his sides. "Isn't that right?" I looked into his eyes once again and let my façade slowly fade away. As far as things had gone now, it was just too much trouble. I reached into the drawer of my writing desk and removed the '*Congratulations*' banner, holding it out across my chest.

"Well done, Mr Wood." I said, folding the banner and placing my hand in my pocket. The banner, I simply laid on my desk. "Oh, what *fun!* I had figured you would be the first to solve my little mystery, albeit a bit early." I picked up my wristwatch that was laying on the desk and looked at the face. "And to be perfectly honest, I was surprised to find that James gave you a run for your money." Mr Wood stood stoic, but I could tell that his eyes conveyed a stunned silence. "I knew he was cleverer than he lets on, but I never realized how useful he would be when a real situation arises."

"Why?" Mr Wood asked. I was disappointed that he didn't have any further philosophy than only a straight question.

"'*Why*'?" I repeated. "Is that all?" I waited for something more, but he just looked at me, expectantly, for elaboration.

"If I may, first, what was it that drew you up here?" I asked. Mr Wood just continued looking at me and finally replied.

"Several things. What you said to Miss Cyrus, for example. That you weren't going to let anyone else die tonight." He began explaining. "To her, that was a relieving promise. The more I thought about it, I realized that everything we found this evening, we were guided to by you. Whatever you said or did, the mystery progressed." I grinned as he put it all together, although I could kick myself for saying what I did to Miss Cyrus. It sent everything off the rails and it left me with an open ending to all my plans. "The card in the shack, the gun in the upstairs room. It was all brought to us by you." I clapped lightly, urging him to continue. "You also said something to Mr Isaac that made him look terrified. Or maybe it was *your* expression that I couldn't see. I had thought it was the fear of his own death that prompted such fear, but it was you that made him look so frightened." He looked down on me, but he looked very small from my perspective. "When I came up here, I began searching your desk for any signs that my theory was right or wrong. Instead, I accidentally brushed a trigger under the left drawer that opened *this*." He gestured at the hidden nook. "I was so upset that I wasn't proven wrong."

"My part of the story." I held up my card from the game. "*The Narrator.*"

"It was you who shot the gardener while you and James were in the garage." He pointed at me.

"And removed one of the professor's bullets to throw a new red herring into the mix." I took my hand from my pocket and showed the bullet I had removed from the gun.

"Why did Mr Langley have to die?" He asked.

"The man was a perfect throwaway pawn on the chessboard. He was never as lazy as he seemed." I began to explain. "Years before he had come to us, Mr Langley was charged with manslaughter. The accidental death of a man he quarrelled with. My aunt found out about it and added him to the blackmail list." Mr Wood kept his firm demeanour but was obviously in rapt attention. "He wouldn't be made a victim, so he didn't refuse to work, he just wouldn't work well for free. I told him that if he did the work he did today, I could release him from the blackmail."

"But you barred him out of the shed so that he would come to you. And you planted the real pistol where Mrs Langley would find it. Under the body?" Mr Wood was in unending awe.

"Of course timing was *everything*." I nodded. "Once I saw him out the front window I rushed to the shed and proceeded to lock up the shed from the inside. I barred the door, shimmied out the window, nailed the window shut and threw the hammer beyond the bushes in the back. After that, I came back inside and began my checks with Mrs Langley in the kitchen. It's as simple as that."

"What made her bring the gun in?"

"Hatred and anger for my aunt? I simply put the weapon in her hand and planned for whatever outcome would occur." I tapped my chin. "However, I expected her to take one of us, hostage, in order to free herself from this house. Then everyone would think it was her until Lady Jilde's death at Mr Isaac's, accidental, hand. And I was surprised to find out that Mr Isaac was the estate's original owner. I guess it's true that you *can* learn something new every day."

"Was this place ever in any real danger?" Mr Wood asked.

"Oh, no. I set all of that up to test my aunt's morality as a slight social experiment some time ago." I chuckled. "I goaded her on by hinting at everyone's secrets. They weren't as subtle as they think when it all comes down to it. And I made some faux documents to seem like the estate was in danger."

"... What did you say?" I could hear the others enter the foyer, their voices confused as to mine and Mr Wood's disappearance. "About goading your aunt?"

"I created the inception of my aunt's blackmail of the others by making passive comments leading her in that direction," I replied to Mr Wood's latest question. "Professor Cole's preferential style; I caught him, once, removing women's makeup. Susan and Andrea's relationship; I always went with them and James to parties, how could I not see it? If James did, *I* certainly could. And of course, Cormac's deception; the man's pathetic lies were so subpar, I really don't even think it requires an explanation."

"Which is why you knew there was no real evidence. But you still haven't answered my real question." Mr Wood growled. I sighed and gave him what it was he wanted.

"All these grand mysteries we study for our entertainment teach us of the genius of a criminal investigation. But people seem to diminish the author's skill at *devising* the perfect crime. Often times it takes a fictional hero like Sherlock Holmes to defeat the unparalleled mind of Professor Moriarty. I was always enthralled with the elusive mastery of the crime, but only when a grander scheme is involved." I grinned.

"So, even you not knowing what you want to do with your life has been a lie?" Mr Wood accused me. I nodded.

"If I were to describe my ambition, I would have to say it is for myself to be the real-life Napoléon of Crime." I laughed. "That sounded less childish in my head, I'll admit." The voices of the others were ascending the stairs. Mr Wood looked over his shoulder and I dove back into my desk, pulling out a spare Derringer pistol I kept in case of an emergency situation. I, then, rushed to the window.

"*Stop!*" Mr Wood shouted. When I turned to him, whilst opening the window, I saw Mrs Cole enter. I gave a warning shot, which I had intended to only hit the door frame. Before getting the mark, the bullet managed to clip the museum director's arm! I had no time to waste and hurried out the window.

Nine

There was no way for me to climb down and use the escape tunnel in the fireplace before the others beat me to the lounge. I had to come out on the ledge, the rain soaking me, as the storm was still on. My wet smoking jacket was beginning to weigh down so I carefully attempted to remove it whilst scaling the side of the manor. I let it drop into the wind and attempted to reach the lattice scaffolding to climb down. I thought I could lose the others in the storm, but my backup plan already had a hiccup. The loud bang of a gunshot echoed in such a way that I had first thought it was thunder until a shingle flew from above me! I looked back to the window and saw Professor Cole, furious, and the gun from his suitcase clutched firmly in his hand. He took two more shots at me. The bullets ricocheted off of the house around me, almost making me lose my footing. I managed to regain my balance, holding tight to the ledge and laughed at the professor's lack of aim. I watched the others pull him in the window and James, then, leaned out with *my* pistol in hand. He pointed the gun that Mrs Langley used on my aunt in my direction.

"You would shoot me, James!?" I called out over the

storm, laughing. "Of all the soul-corrupting things you do, could you kill as well?" I laughed once again.

"My friend? No." He called back. "A murderer? Yes!"

"Then let me make it easy for you!" I outstretched my arm and hung outward in a flamboyant pose, making my torso a perfect target for him. I could immediately sense his hesitation.

"I *will* shoot you, Jon!" He yelled. "Now, come back inside, so we can take you to the authorities!"

"Actions speak louder than words, old friend!" I gave one last triumphant laugh before something inexplicable happened. An act of God, maybe? If He *is* real, I could see it being the reason for what happened to me next.

As I leaned out, my Derringer in my un-bracing hand, a lightning strike connected with the gunmetal and, subsequently, to the rest of myself! I had been smote with a bolt of lightning and fell from the second floor! My earlier statements of out of body experiences were, of course, utter bull. But this time, I really *was* looking down upon myself as I fell through the rain. Time seemed to slow the further down I got. I couldn't believe the result of this evening. It was incredible. I got to spend the evening being a *brilliant* criminal mastermind, fooling some of the greatest minds I know. True, Mr Wood found me out, but for a beginner, I'd say I did very well. The sole architect of multiple blackmail cases, five murders, the fall of an aristocrat and her faith. I was an unparalleled puppet master! I even became the owner of an entire estate through my actions. And many say that crime does not pay.

After what felt like an eternal fall, I landed in the gardens below, which brings my narration to an abrupt end. I blacked out upon reaching the flowerbeds, although, I could swear I was unconscious earlier than that. All I remember seeing, in the end, was the clouds parting and the moon shining bright as the rain surrounded my body.

The others made their way outside to bring me in. With the storm having dissipated, at long last, James left the manor with Mr Wood to go down the hill and retrieve the authorities in the latter's car. It was so sudden, the way it all came to a screeching end. Being the mastermind was the greatest thrill of my life! Yet already I was missing the charge I felt from being the author of an entire storyline. On top of that, my time to reflect made me realize that I can't ever be satisfied with my first and *only* work. So much to do in such a short life. They had brought me in through the French doors and laid me out in the foyer, adjacent to Mrs Langley.

"I can't believe this." Susan stood next to the front door, staring out the window.

"He had us all fooled, Susan." Spencer was laid out on the couch in the lounge with ice wrapped in a towel on his head.

"Any more than we've fooled ourselves?" She asked. "Thinking we can all keep our secrets." The sounds of sirens wailed at the bottom of the hill. "They're here." Susan stated.

"Question is, how will they get up here?" Andrea queried.

"*C'est vrai*, there is that massive hole to consider." Amelia took a look out of the lounge window and sighed.

"Mrs Cole, please." Miss Cyrus pleaded. Essie was trying to clean the wound on the art director's arm.

"*Ne t'en fais pas,* Essie, it is a scratch." Mrs Cole waved at Miss Cyrus. "I just want to see how they are faring down the hill. My arm is not going to fall off in that time." She joked, prompting a relieving laugh from the maid.

It seemed to take no time at all for the police and ambulance to arrive in the courtyard of the estate. As soon as Mrs Cole turned around she saw them all pulling in, avoiding the already parked cars. Susan opened the door for the authorities, who came with James and Mr Wood in tow.

"How did you get here so quickly?" Susan asked them.

"We told them that we would need to cross a hole." James

explained. "We got some large panels of wood and laid them across the gap."

"Although, we did have to clear some of the limbs out of it." Mr Wood said as he stood over my covered body. The medical examiner went to work checking me, as I was the only non-dead body to be looked at.

"So, what happened here?" One of the officers asked as his colleagues spread about the house.

"How much time do you have?" James scoffed.

"I don't believe it!" The paramedic cried, grasping every-one's attention. "You said this man fell from the second-floor window?"

"He did, yes," James confirmed for the man. "Just after get-ting struck by lightning."

"Impossible!" The medic exclaimed. "He's still *alive* and there's barely a scratch on him! There's a possibility of some contusions, but no burns or scorches."

"Not even on his hand? It struck the gun clutched in his right hand." Mr Wood described, kneeling next to me. He uncovered my hand and it seemed untouched until he turned it over. He aided the medical examiner in opening my hand and noticed that my palm was, indeed, burned.

"Incredible!" The medic took a look at my hand. "There is no way he should even *be* alive."

"You should send him to the hospital and keep him guarded until he wakes... *If* he wakes..." Mr Wood suggested.

My friends succeeded in bringing in the architect of a perfect crime. I was taken by the medical ambulance, given I had yet to wake from my comatose state. During my on-site examination, the paramedics and the others were shocked that I, myself, was not dead after a bolt of lightning and a two-story fall. Pure luck that I managed to fall in the garden beds, I suppose. But even *I* couldn't say how I managed to survive the bolt of pure electricity with only a scarred palm to show for it. It hardly matters. Had I been awake, I would have been tried and hanged for my extensive crimes. I was exactly where I needed to be. Placed in a secured hospital wing. And thus, my part in this story is done... but the story is not yet over.

Ten

Oxford's extensive streets house many buildings newly owned by Roland Wood. One such sizable housing can be found on Holywell Street. A Victorian building, situated between a bookstore and a bakery. It was this house that Essie Cyrus had been called to by Mr Wood. Miss Cyrus shuffled nervously on the sidewalk and double-checked the address on the letter she'd received. It was the right place. She walked up to the stoop beyond the small metal gate, glancing at the new metal plaque that read '*Everjust*'. Essie hesitated but knocked on the door and folded her hands around the letter. Essie had been making up for lost funds these last few weeks by washing dishes and bussing tables in a pub. She remained lost in thought until she heard the door latch rattle. Essie jolted to attention and stood up straight, brushing off her shabby coat. When the door opened there stood a young man with well-combed black hair and a dark suit, perfectly poised with a kindly face. He was so well kept, he almost didn't look like a real person. No wrinkle or crease in his suit and a posture only seen on statues.

"Miss Essie Cyrus?" The man asked. His accent was very northern and upper class. He reached into his vest pocket and pulled out an obsessively polished fob watch. He flicked open the face and peered down at it. He frowned a bit, not losing any of the softness of his face. "You are four minutes and twenty-three seconds late." He said, clapping the watch shut again. He stepped to the side and held out his hand, gesturing Miss Cyrus in. She did as instructed and entered the small foyer area. "Very good. Come now, don't dawdle." He said, leading her into a sizable living room where the walls were lined with bookshelves. The room was finely furnished and the ceiling carried a beautiful chandelier. The drapes over the windows were shuttered but a window seat was visible from under them.

"Um... Mister-" Essie began.

"Blackbird, ma'am. Cecil Blackbird." The man said.

"Mr Blackbird. Where is Mr Wood?" Essie asked. "I was asked to-"

"Come here to speak with Roland about something that may be of great interest to you, personally." He explained, his soft smile returning. "I typed up the letter myself, Miss." He bowed. Cecil took out his watch, once again. "As for where he is, likely mucking up my schedule to no end."

"Calm yourself, Cecil." Mr Wood entered, finishing with his tie. "A few minutes awry won't end the entire world."

"Mr Wood!" Essie exclaimed. She was happy to see a friendly face that she actually recognized.

"Essie!" Mr Wood walked over and bent over to hug the young maid. She embraced her tall friend and the two stepped back to a measure of decorum. "I suppose you're wondering why I've asked you here?"

"Yes. Very much so." She replied with a nod.

"I've purchased this home to be my living place whenever I'm in town." He gestured as he began to explain. "It will also serve as the meeting place for the Criminology Society."

"I see." Miss Cyrus was confused as to what this had to do with her.

"That being said, I am away on business quite often and I need the place kept up with." Mr Wood continued to explain. "Cecil is very methodical, but he is still only *one* man." If Essie had been sitting she would have been on the edge of her seat. "He will need help keeping this place orderly and I could think of none better than the best maid I've ever seen."

"You want to hire me on?" Essie bounced on her heels.

"That *is* what the point of calling you here was." Cecil added.

"This house will be your home." Mr Wood explained. "Unlike the Jilde estate, you will have decent living quarters."

He turned to the young butler. "Cecil, will you take Miss Cyrus upstairs to her room?"

"Miss Cyrus?" Cecil motioned her to follow him with a bow. Essie looked up at Mr Wood, unable to convey how thankful she was. He didn't need to hear it. He could see it in her eyes, and he replied to her expression with a smile and a nod. "Come *along*, please!" Cecil called from the staircase snapping his fingers. "So much to do in so little time." Essie hurried to follow the impatient horologist.

The upstairs looked just as ornate as the dining room at the Jilde estate. The biggest difference, however, was the more inviting colour of the walls. The paper was a gorgeous light blue with deco patterns. Much more modern and updated than the Victorian manor. Mr Wood had done some fast work to settle into the house. The top of the staircase was an open vestibule that looked like another foyer with a table in the centre. There were two doors immediately on either end of the large landing and a hallway straight ahead. The floor also continued on from the right door down toward the front of the house. The bannister lead to another door and a large window situated in an alcove above where the front door would be.

"My room." Cecil pointed to the door on the right. "Roland's, attic entrance and empty room, renovation pending." He pointed down the hallway. "Loo, bath included." He pointed to the room on the left then turned to the room next to the alcove. "Your room." He waved her to follow. Essie did so, enamoured with the incredible architecture so much that she hadn't even recognized that this would be her new home. Cecil opened the door for her and inside was a much more generous room than her previous home! It had the same blue wallpaper with gothic moulding and more furnishing than she has ever used in her life! A large bed with soft covers, a vanity counter, and a huge armoire! There was more to be seen in the room, but Miss Cyrus could hardly see it through her tears of sheer joy. She was standing, hand to mouth as Cecil entered the room to open her wardrobe.

"Mr Blackbird?" She choked out.

"Cecil will do, Miss." He replied to her as he took a new maid uniform out for her and hung it on the coat rack next to the wardrobe. "Your new uniform. You'll have the rest of today to get settled in. I expect you up bright and early to receive your list of duties in the kitchen. Downstairs, behind the staircase and to the left. Avoid the dining room, as it is also under renovation, please." Miss Cyrus nodded, barely able to catch up to the hurried young butler's instruction. "Very good. The Coles will be in tomorrow, so I expect your best foot forward for our friends."

"Yes, sir!" Essie stood straight and smiled after wiping her tears away.

"Again, just Cecil will do." He replied, walking past her. "Be sure to see me at the end of every week. I will be providing your pay to you and Cook. Your days off will be each Monday. Mr Wood will be away next week, so-" He continued his list, but Essie was barely listening. She was so happy that she didn't have to simply get by any longer. She could actually *live*. She could be *alive*.

Mr Wood, still down in the parlour, poured a cup of tea for himself. He picked up the paper and placed it on the table next to his seat. With a yawn, he returned to prepping his tea. As he poured the cream he saw Cecil come down the stairs and into the parlour.

"Settling in." The butler replied before his employer could ask, peering once again at his watch.

"Care for a cuppa?" Mr Wood offered.

"Not just now. I still have a few errands to run, and this business with Miss Cyrus has put me back fifteen minutes." Cecil explained, putting his watch back in his vest.

"Suit yourself." Mr Wood shrugged. Cecil left the house after donning his bowler hat, a pair of cheaters and an overcoat, leaving Mr Wood to handle himself. He took a sip of his tea and walked out into the foyer. "Hm." He looked up to be sure that Miss Cyrus was not in earshot. Mr Wood walked around behind the stairs and removed the phone from the hook to dial a number.

"Warneford Hospital." A voice said on the other end.

"My name is Roland Wood. I'm calling to inquire about the condition of a coma patient." He asked.

"Uh, we only have one." The young lady on the hospital's end said. "A Mr Jonathan Everard."

"Yes, I'm the primary benefactor behind his care. I wondered if there was any change in his condition." Mr Wood inquired.

"Let me just check with the doctor." Said the receptionist. "Please hold."

Mr Wood waited patiently. He reflected on what had transpired that night. He had known Jonathan since he was a boy. Mr Wood could never come to terms with the fact that the kind, quiet, clever boy he had mentored had grown to become criminally insane. Even more so, Lady Integra Jilde, who he had known for years, was far more piteous. Mr Wood's judgement was clouded by the fact that they were so close to him. He never even saw the signs of blackmail or murderous intent and nothing ever got past him? Could it be that Roland was losing his edge? He was snapped from his thoughts when the doctor picked up.

"Hello? Doctor Zilchrist speaking." A man on the other end of the phone spoke with an exotic accent.

"Oh, good day, Doctor." Mr Wood shook off his thoughts. "This is Mr Roland Wood. I was calling to inquire on the condition of Jonathan Everard."

"I see." The doctor retorted, his tone flat but not dismal. "He is still in his comatose state. No difference aside from his breathing getting better."

"And his hand?" Mr Wood asked.

"Ah, the burns. The skin will be permanently scarred, but if he doesn't wake up it will hardly make a difference." The doctor sighed.

"I understand. I believe that covers my inquiry." Mr Wood concluded. "Thank you, Doctor Zilchrist." They bid each other a good day and Mr Wood sighed once more.

"Mr Wood?" Essie called from the foyer. Again, he was snapped out of his dismal thoughts and peered around the corner.

"Yes, Essie?" He called back. She turned his way and smiled.

"I'll be back soon! I'm going to go and retrieve the few things I own." She bobbed on her feet, eager to run out the door so she could return.

Mr Wood smiled. The look on Essie's face reassured him.

He hadn't lost his touch, he was just a victim of his own human error. He was never arrogant, but this experience would ensure that he never would be. Mr Wood would need to stay humble since he was now the sole head of the intrepid group of Haut Monde misfits, the Criminology Society.

Epilogue

The doctor hung up the phone and scratched his stubbled cheek. He shook his head and walked back into the hospital to do his rounds. Dr Zilchrist had checked on three patients, but something else kept preying on his mind. The curious patient that gave the hospital so much recent notoriety. The doctor walked the halls, deep in his thoughts, until he realized he was next to the door of one Mr Everard. Me. When he entered the room it was just myself and the nurse.

"Nurse?" Dr Zilchrist asked. She turned around with a start. "Everything alright?"

"Yes, doctor." The woman stated. "I was getting ready to turn down the bed."

"I'll fetch the gurney for you to get the patient over. Sorry for the scare." He said. The doctor paused at the door. "You haven't noticed any changes in the patient, have you?"

"No, doctor. Why do you ask? Have you?" The nurse queried back to him.

"I only ask because you've spent quite a bit of time with this patient." He raised his brow.

"Well, as I was told, he was to remain under constant supervision. If at any point he wakes, the authorities are to be called." She listed the instructions perfectly.

"Very good." Dr Zilchrist stated with a smile and a nod. He proceeded to leave and get the gurney and some orderlies to aid in moving me.

Once I was sure he was out of earshot I chuckled and sat up in my bed. His cluelessness was comical to me. I'll need to keep a closer eye on him than he keeps on me. I glanced over to my nurse, standing at attention next to my bed. I had managed to put the sweet woman in my employ by proving to her that I could gain access to her family at night when there is much less security. Or I could pay her well with more money than she could dream. Unbeknownst to Mr Wood, I could skim funds from my new fortune by sending her to the bank to collect. No one would ever suspect the coma patient or his matronly nurse.

"Well done, my dear." I cleared my throat. Feigning a coma makes it hard on the throat from disuse. "We'll need to watch him. The doctor is beginning to grow suspicious."

"I don't think that he'll be a problem." My nurse spoke. "As long as I steer him away, he'll never find out."

"A master never leaves things to chance." I put my hands together and sat in thought.

"What will happen?" She asked with growing concern. Without a doubt, she was afraid that I would ask her to do something about the doctor.

"Nothing that need concern you." I placed my hands on my lap and leaned over the side of the bed. My back was incredibly stiff which prompted a groan from me. "My journal, please." The nurse knelt down and pulled a leatherbound journal from beneath the mattress. She handed it over along with a pen from her apron. "Thank you. Now, what do you have for me?"

"Mr Wood has moved into and is renovating a house on Holywell Street. He intends to call it '*Everjust*'." I laughed at the idea of Mr Wood naming his new home after me. A way of commemorating that fateful night to remind the Society of what I'd done. I found it touching. "In addition, he asked your maid to come into his employ." She reported.

"Ah, that sounds like Mr Wood. I'm glad someone is looking out for Miss Cyrus." I said as I continued to jot down my notes. She regaled me with most of the details from the final chapter. Yes, the '*ending*' of my narration was another lie. Apologies. My nurse was to be my confidante to the outside world and keep tabs on my old friends. She would also be my primary networker to those I thought might be useful in my journey to become a master criminal, as well. I *would* become the true-life Napoléon of Crime. And someday I know my path will cross again with the Criminology Society. I am so excited. End of entry.

Photo by J.L. Dumire

J.L. Dumire is a new author building a career in what he enjoys most - entertaining fiction. Currently a retail worker, he hopes to build a career allowing him time to devote to his loved ones and entertaining others. J.L. has two particular favorites in fiction: Urban Fantasy, depicting magic and mythology in a modern setting; and Mystery, which most children are introduced to by watching *Scooby-Doo*. J.L. Dumire's love of mysteries began with *Murder She Wrote* when he was barely out of diapers.